AN ANAGRAM FOR GOODBYE

AN ANAGRAM FOR GOODBYE

ROCK NEELLY

ISBN: 978-1-958414-24-8

Goshen, Kentucky 40026

Enigma House Press

www.enigmahousepress.com

To the wonderful women in my life, including granddaughters Anna and Lucy, stepdaughter Kara, my mother Peggy, and my wonderful wife, Vicki. I love you all.

I know what happens—I read the book.
I believe I just got the goodbye look.
-Donald Fagen

THE DIRTY FORTUNE COOKIE

The phone call arrived only one week into my forced retirement—seven days after Roddy had thrown me out of my own detective agency. Not that I didn't deserve it. He said he could no longer trust me. I understood. I wasn't so sure I could trust myself. In life-and-death confrontations, you have to be sure of yourself—and your partner—and I wasn't to be trusted. Therefore, stand down, old boy. Stand down.

But knowing does not make doing any easier. I mean, I'm forty-four. And benched. What do you call that? Untrustworthy. Unreliable. Roddy said he couldn't trust me to have his back. Roddy had called me unreliable. That would be okay if he just continued to call me. Being forgotten was worse than being unreliable. That preyed upon my mind. I sat there for a week, just waiting for the phone to ring. For Roddy to say he forgave me. But there was silence. No calls. Just me and the coyote in the trailer out in Topanga Canyon. The two of us staring at my cell phone. Waiting. Hoping someone would jingle my jangle.

Then someone did. Linda. Linda called and asked for my help. Linda.

I agreed to her evening request, hearing the sound of her voice for the first time in at least a decade. It was instantly recognizable, more world-weary, but still a siren's song to me. I said I would see her the next afternoon. Linda.

Linda.

But there were things which needed to be done before I drove down to Orange County. I resolved to get to bed early and be down from the hills before Los Angeles traffic was at full snarl. I awoke before dawn, put on coffee, and cooked two sausage patties. Mine, I put on toast, the second I busted up and mixed with scrambled eggs for Dapper, my pet coyote. He wagged his tail with appreciation.

Far up here in Topanga Canyon, the only neighbors I now have are coyotes and pot farmers—*and* there are fewer marijuana cultivators in the hills since legalization, to be honest. So mainly coyotes and me. Both Dapper and I have rejected our packs—or been rejected by them. We just hang together, the two of us, the Topanga Rejects. A pair of lone wolves. But today, with the sun coming up, I left him and headed down the canyon toward the big bad city. Dapper, who now uses a dog door on my Airstream trailer home, didn't bother to come outside to see me off. He merely raised his head from the air-conditioned, vented comfort of his bed to acknowledge my departure. He is officially spoiled.

Roddy opened the door with a yawn. He still wore compression shorts sewn tight below his stumps and a t-shirt that announced, "The Hold Steady Nearly Killed Me!" Rod was not yet on his stilts—protheses are for later in the day, and, Lyle Lovett says, "Pants is overrated."

"Come on in," Rod said, his voice still raspy with sleep. "Jerry just made some coffee."

Jerry is his pet monkey. Jerry can talk, using gorilla sign language prompts on an audible device strapped to his left arm stump. He too is missing a limb.

"I'm glad to see Hollywood fame hasn't spoiled Jer."

"I wouldn't go that far," Roddy said, smiling, thinking of last week when his pet monkey had been on both *The Today Show* and *The Tonight Show with Jimmy Fallon* the same day. Cra-cra times. "I am ordering Jerry new pants off Amazon because he's definitely too big for his britches these days." He said the last sentence loudly, but Jerry ignored us.

"What brings you down the mountain?" Roddy asked.

"I took a case."

"Damn it, Grace," Roddy admonished, "you said you would stand down. That is a bad idea."

"Let me explain."

Rod did—after he poured me a cup.

Linda Martin had been Linda Hendrix when I met her. That was long ago before the turn of the century. I was in the police academy, training to become an officer in the LAPD. The program to be a cop is a six-month ordeal. It is rigorous, and I was gung-ho. My brother went into the Navy immediately after high school. Two years later, I left home after receiving an Associates at San Francisco State. I took one year of studies at USC. However, accounting was too staid and boring. My father was a cop. My brother was in the service – now the CIA. A need for adrenalin was in our blood, my mother claimed. Two days after turning 21, I decided to join the thin blue line. I studied hard at the academy, deciding to stay in L.A.

But I was twenty-one in a city filled with women wanting to become movie stars. Police cadets did some drinking, frequenting water holes catering to newly arrived, undiscovered beauties. I was among the horny boys in blue—at least most Saturday nights. I can't say I found any stars—or beauties until one Sunday morning.

Most weekends, mildly hungover, we would have breakfast at the L.A. Police Revolver and Athletic Club Café. And yes, that is a real thing. That is where I first saw Linda. I fell in love at first sight. Unfortunately, I saw her two seconds after my study buddy and roommate at the academy, Landaugh Martin did. Martin was the star of our cadet class. He was leading man handsome with a great shock of blonde hair, angular face, and chiseled chin. He was tall, lanky, and athletic. And supremely confident. When I met him, I believe every eligible woman who ever met him tried to get him to choose her from the mob. Landaugh always had the pick of the litter. It made him intolerable on the subject of women, but that confidence made him a great partner at the police academy. We lived together, studied together, ran together. Hell, we were always together. Landaugh just happened to see Linda before I did.

"Look at *her*," he said, looking up from his omelet.

I did. My breath caught. Linda was filling a cup of coffee, waitressing on the side as she worked on her social work degree at Cal State Long Beach. She looked like a Beach Boys video. Long blonde hair tied up in a ponytail, thin, tanned, long-legged, and with a perfect face. She wore a prim white waitressing apron over a pin-striped navy shirt and skirt. Her blue eyes eventually turned to us, feeling our eyes on her. Linda blushed and turned to the kitchen, pretending she didn't see us staring.

Before we had left, Landaugh had worked his magic. Linda had agreed to go to dinner that evening with him. Strangely, he invited me along.

For the remainder of academy training until graduation, the three of us were inseparable. Ours was a small two-bedroom apartment, but it soon housed three. I can't say I loved her from afar. She was always right there. When we were awarded our badges, Linda was there in the audience. I could hear her cheer when I shook the Police Chief's hand. I noted her call of praise was louder for Landaugh than for me. It caused an ache that I never told anyone about – not until a night many years later with Roddy and I on a stake-out, spilling our guts about lost love.

Soon, Landaugh and I received our postings. I was assigned South Central in the 'hood. Landaugh received a punch to the gut—the Harbor Area, as far south as you could get, nowhere near close enough to sniff Los Angeles' cool vibe. His precinct was in San Pedro. His face fell when he saw it on the board the day the listings came out. But he had Linda and I didn't. I would have traded my beat for her in a flash. Landaugh and Linda were married within six months of our graduation. I was, of course, best man, and their wedding day was a tough day for me—I wanted happiness for her, but to toast them, the two of them, pained me. Linda was the one who got away.

Landaugh joined the Chips after the minimum time he could spend in blue. Riding a motorcycle was more his style. Riding two wheels, he was always in the middle of the action. Landaugh took chances. He was highly decorated. I got word from people who knew I was his friend that Landaugh was incredibly popular with the rank-and-file, but also made enemies with brass above him.

I also heard he was a womanizer. It killed me to know he was stepping out on Linda. That was the biggest part of why I let them go. Being around them when I knew of his infidelity created such turmoil for me. Seeing her try so hard to keep Landaugh close pained me. I tried to stop thinking about her. About them. I ghosted them before that was even a verb.

Until I received a birth announcement in the mail. By this time, years had passed. I now wore a gold shield and was a detective. I partnered with Janelle Jackson. It was 2000. I looked at the photo inside of the card when it arrived—Landaugh, Linda, and Nev, their daughter, all happy-like. I sent an expensive throw from Elfin in Woodland Hills, but I didn't go see them.

Landaugh was, by then, a Sergeant in the Chips. However, the rumor mill about him, when I heard something, which was not often, was that his eventual promotion had been hampered by both his reputation as a loose cannon and his refusal to get off his bike. He did not want a desk job. I got that. The seat of a motorcycle is more fun than the seat of LAPD desk chair.

"I know all of this," Roddy said, interrupting my tale. "But now both Landaugh and the daughter are dead, right?"

"Presumed dead," I corrected. "Their bodies were never found."

"Didn't the police find a van with their blood inside? Verified by DNA. I read about it in the papers while you were gone. The bank robbery was major news."

"Yeah, I was gone, evading jihad during all of that," I said. I stood and freshened my coffee cup. I nodded at Rod's. He nodded in turn. I topped off his too.

"What's Jerry doing?" I asked, deflecting.

"Studying lines with his reader/roller. He's got a pizza commercial filming tomorrow. Gracie is still asleep. She's in a growth spurt. Karen left before it got light."

I smiled. Gracie, his daughter, was turning three soon. I was her godfather and she was named after me.

"Not knowing what became of Landaugh and Nev is killing Linda. She wants me to find out what happened," I said.

Rod made a face. "Look, I get it. You had the hots for this

woman twenty years ago. You came in second. She married somebody else. Maybe she made a bad choice, but now she's widowed. You want to be her knight in shining armor. I get all that. But you should not be in the field. You killed somebody. You made me hide a murder."

I nodded, knowing I was just there to inform him, not to ask for permission. Roddy knew me better than anyone. He saw the look in my eyes.

"You going to do this no matter what I say, right?"

"Yeah, I might need help with computers and access. Can I count on you?"

"Just so we're clear, you are just reviewing police reports and such. Not carrying a weapon. Can't have you killing any more neo-Nazi assholes, can we?"

I smiled. "Never say never."

Roddy laughed. "Wrong answer."

I met Linda that afternoon. Time had been kind to her. She was still lean and graceful. Her face was still angular, incredibly beautiful, but there was a sadness there I had not known in her. Of course, I knew the cause.

She marveled at my notoriety, Roddy's and my fame—or infamy—as the Purple Heart Detectives. She asked kindly about my lost leg, saying she knew about phantom limb pain and its trauma.

I was in love again before she served lunch. Eventually, she tried to seal the deal.

"Will you do it? Will you try to find out what happened to them?"

"Of course, but I don't know if I can help. The police always make a big deal when one of their own is involved. No expense was spared, I'm sure. No lead not explored. No leaf left unturned."

"Landaugh *was not* on the force at the time of the bank robbery, and he stepped on a lot of toes when he *was* on watch."

"That was just Landaugh. Those of us who knew him well..." I didn't finish.

Linda smiled kindly, watching me try to say only pleasant things. She had heard the talk too.

"Landaugh banged up his hip in the motorcycle accident and took full disability two years before," I said, filling the silence that had fallen.

Linda nodded. "Yes, Lanny had hip replacement, but he still limped. It was worse after sitting which always seemed strange to me. Afterwards, he took a security job at the Carson Citizen's Bank because it required him to stand. I hated it for him. A man so in need of speed to suddenly stop and be in the lobby of a bank for hours at a time. But Lanny seemed resolved to make it work. He said he didn't mind the standing. Just wouldn't sit at a desk."

"Did you need the money?"

"Not so much. He had a full pension, but Nev had turned eighteen. She was in college. We couldn't really afford for her to go away, so she went to Cal State. Landaugh built Nev her own apartment above the garage with a separate entrance from the alleyway to give her some independence. She was studying nursing, second year."

"Your own alma mater."

"Yes, and of course, we had my income. I'm now head of the Orange County Hospital's social services department. My income is good, but you know...." Her voice trailed off.

I let her drift into silence again and just watched her. The silence extended, but this time it didn't feel awkward. I saw her blink, surprised by the sudden intimacy. She shrugged it off, trying to consciously thwart it.

"So how will you start?" Linda asked.

"Police reports. Film footage of the robbery. Can you tell me the detective in charge of the case?"

"Fernando Vega," she said. "He's still on the job. He's good. He did all he could. I will call him and ask him to give you access to whatever you need."

Fernando Vega was a small man, but my first reaction was I would not want to cross him. His intense eyes reviewed me as he handed me files and a flash drive.

"She's a good lady," he said. "Been through a lot. I would hate to see her hurt."

"I know," I said, trying to reassure him. "I've known her forever. I was best man at their wedding. I don't know if there is anything I can do, but she asked. I told her I would take a look. Couldn't say no."

Vega only nodded.

"I won't waste your time," I said.

Vega nodded again, handed me the files, and went back to work.

The police report was nothing if not thorough. Three people entered the bank with weapons and masks—two men and one woman. Bank employees did as they were told, following protocol. However, Landaugh Martin, one of two guards on duty at that time, suddenly began to participate in the robbery, assisting the three armed assailants. Landaugh told the other guard, a Norman Wickers, that the bank robbers held his daughter and would kill her unless he helped them.

The bank was just down the street from the nation's largest maker of Fiberglas boat hulls. Twelve hundred employees received their Christmas bonus on the first of December each year. A preponderance would cash their check when the plant closed that Friday. In anticipation of those cash withdrawals, the bank carried an extra million in green that day.

The robbers were in and out in less than three minutes. The take was more than two million dollars. Strangely, as I watched the recording, Landaugh seemed a bit too eager as I reviewed the footage. He even pistol-whipped a bank V.P. who hesitated giving access to the vault. I studied Landaugh's face, but it gave away little. It had been so long since I knew him. I could no longer read his thoughts.

The robbers were disguised, but one was tall and thin, perhaps 6-4, the second man just under six feet, the woman, thin and roughly 5-9. They all wore coveralls, baseball caps, gloves, and Wayfarers. Hair color of all three was red, like Dennis the Menace red. The FBI had established all wore wigs. Identification would be difficult.

Upon exiting the bank, the four, including Landaugh, piled into a van and departed the scene. Despite police arriving within two minutes after the bank robbers' escape, the van's route was never established. Street cameras did not find the vehicle. Neither did helicopters prowling for them within ten minutes. They just disappeared.

However, the van was found a couple of months later, drifted halfway up the wheel wells in a remote part of the eastern Mojave Desert near the Tehachapi Mountains. FBI technicians found blood traces of Nev in the grooves of the rear door foot plate. Landaugh's blood was found inside the bracing on the side entry door. No bodies were found. Investigators believed the bodies were dumped elsewhere and van discarded at a secondary location.

I studied the files for two days. I watched the bank robbery video fifty times. Nothing leaped out at me. I met Linda and told her I was stymied.

"So that's it?"

"No, that's just the end of the beginning. I'll try to see if the criminal class of Southern California has any news about the robbery. I'll talk to the other bank guard, Norman Wickers. I'll check with the FBI to see if any of the money ever showed up on the street, although Landaugh guided the robbers to not take the traceable bills or the paint packets. Most of the cash taken was untraceable."

Linda nodded and gave me a hug, which I lingered in too

long. With one extra tight squeeze, she released her arms and left me to my devices.

"Detective Pancake? I heard you was retired."

I laughed. "The news of my demise has been greatly exaggerated."

I was speaking to the oldest gangbanger in L.A., Thiago Reyes. He calls me "Detective Pancake," because, you know, "I hop."

"You back in the game? Making the world safe for multinational gunrunners?"

"No, nothing like that anymore, but I am working on something. Thought you might provide me a solid," I said into my burner phone. I was glad Thiago still had the same secret number.

"My policy is to assist when I can, but you got to scratch my back too," Reyes cackled his answer.

"You need something?"

"I'll think on it. For now, what you need?"

"I'm working on the Carson Citizens bank job from two years back. Trying to find the guard and his daughter."

"That old news," he said. "Trying to find their bones out in the Mojave more likely."

I winced. "Yeah, that could be the result. But the widow wants to know. Bury her own."

"I get that. People need to close the book on things before they move on."

"Yeah, they do. Did you ever hear anything about the three who went in? They walked out with two million. You would think there would be talk on the street for a score like that."

"Yeah, we wanted to know, but there was nothing. It wasn't anybody we'd heard of. Nobody local like. Out of town talent, we always figured. One in and done."

"Okay, you want to put a word on the street? I'll pay a reward for info."

"How much?"

"For a real lead that gets me a step closer? I think we can go five grand."

"Ten and I'll personally put the word out."

"Deal."

I spoke to the bank guard. Norman Wickers. He remembered little about the whole robbery. I suspected the onset of dementia. He only said one thing that struck me as true.

"Landaugh Martin always acted like he was too good for the rest of us. I heard they took his daughter, but right when it happened, I thought it was just like him. Spit in our faces, you know?"

The FBI was no help. Not that they ever are. They are like spoiled brats at a Montessori School who won't share the toys. I finally talked to a case officer who volunteered one factoid—no money from the crime had ever been found. None of the marked bills were ever retired by the treasury.

"How many marked bills were there?"

"Out of the two million taken?"

"Yeah," I said, impatiently.

"Just two thousand dollars, mostly in twenties. There were ten thousand more, but the bank guard, ex-cop, knew which stacks were the traceable bills. Robbers left them behind. Dye packs too."

"Thanks."

"Think he was involved?" Agent Brat asked.

"What?" I asked, surprised at this breach into actual human interaction. "What makes you say that?"

"Perfect crime. Those always seem to have an inside man."

"Maybe an unwilling one."

"Maybe." And he then was gone, the federal government always glad to assist.

With no idea of what to do next, I went to see Linda. I asked her if I could see Nev's room and look through her belongings.

"Why? The police looked. They didn't find anything. The bank robbers appear to have taken her hostage after she left for classes before the robbery. There was no note. No nothing. Just what Landaugh told the teller about Nev during the robbery. And of course," Linda paused, "the blood spot."

"Certainly, but that tiny speck of blood does not indicate

massive blood loss. It just shows she was in that van. That's about it."

"I know."

"Maybe after I look over her apartment, I'll look at her computer footprint."

The police still had Nev's computer, but Linda said I could peruse Nev's email accounts and her social media sites. "Detective Vega—and me—have looked through emails and texts a million times," she said, "There's nothing there."

"Probably not, but I'll look. A fresh set of eyes never hurts."

Linda gave me the email address and password. Next, she took me to Nev's room above the garage. She assured me it was just as her daughter left it. That, at least, was good news.

It was a typical studio apartment and could have been above any store front in Southern California, except here it was above Landaugh's and Linda's garage. The garage structure itself was a standalone. The entrance for three cars was at the rear of the property. The door to the apartment was from inside the garage; however, a second exit, required for residences in Los Angeles County, was a fire escape stairway down the back, into the smallish backyard.

Linda stood there at the fire escape stairway after she let me in. I asked her to go back to the house and make coffee. I would be back to her within the hour. She left reluctantly and I began to prowl.

I found no diary and certainly no smoking gun. However, one thing piqued my curiosity. On the refrigerator, Nev had taped several fortunes taken from fortune cookies. They were about as dirty as I could remember seeing:

"You will soon get kisses in unexpected places."

"Nookie or cookie?"

"You're only as old as you feel. Can I feel you?"

In the bathroom, more were taped to the mirror:

"Your tongue is your ambassador."

"Your smile is a curve that can get something straight for me."

"Pigeon poop burns the retina for 13 hours. You will learn this lesson the hard way."

That one made me laugh.

The last one, taped to her make-up mirror, was ominous:

"Sex is a killer. Want to die happy?"

That one looked easy to pry off the curved surface. I did. On the back, besides the expected lucky numbers, a small code was printed in the right corner. I put my phone camera on the tiny print and zoomed in. It read "Made by DFCAT." Hmmm.

Looking around the apartment, there was little to note. A film of dust covered all the surfaces. There was no phone, little correspondence, just old magazines, and no connection to anyone else. Connections for a nineteen-year-old are conducted by phone or by laptop. Nev's phone had never been recovered. The police had the laptop.

In the tiny pantry, I found something interesting. A tin labeled "Dirty Fortune Cookies." They were manufactured by DFCAT, Austin, Texas.

I retreated to the house to find Linda. She poured me a cup of coffee.

"Did you find anything?"

"Probably not," I said, "but I am curious. Did Nev ever go

to Austin? To the festival, South-by-Southwest or something?"

"Oh yes, her best friend. Mabs, Mabel Freeman, is going to school at the University of Texas. With Nev having to stay at home, we gave her money to visit Austin a couple times. I guess to get a bit of the college experience, being on her own. Spending time with Mabs." Linda smiled over the rim of her cup, having the fond memory. "Why did you ask?"

"Oh, the fortune cookies."

"Yes," Linda said, rolling her eyes. "Awful, aren't they?"

"Did she ever eat there?"

"In Austin?"

"No, sorry," I said, "at a restaurant called The Dirty Fortune Cookie?"

Linda seemed confused. "Maybe, I don't know. What difference could that possibly make?"

"Did she meet someone out there?"

"No, I don't think—I mean no one she mentioned. I'm sure Mabs has friends. They were underaged, but they drank. I mean, so did we at that age."

"Can I have Mabs' number?'

Mabs was now a senior and a busy young woman. It took several unsuccessful call attempts and finally a text from Linda before the girl returned my call. Mabs was evasive, but eventually I learned that Nev had met a man out there. A musician named Jack Frost.

"Did he play at the Dirty Fortune Cookie?"

"No, that's a Chinese place, mainly takeout. He played up the street at Ziggy's Martian Tavern."

"Bowie reference," I said. "Cool."

"What?" Mabs replied, confirming my age and my ancient pop culture references.

"Never mind. Is Jack Frost still around?"

"No," Mabs said, "he went to L.A. to see Nev two or three times before she went missing, but then he came back for about a week. The club changed management, I heard, and they replaced him with a reggae band. I mean, that made more sense with the Ziggy reference, right? I heard Jack and the band moved to L.A. to get a record contract."

I thanked her and ended the call.

Linda asked if I found out anything. I told her I was going to Austin in the morning.

Austin is thirty square miles surrounded by reality, but I love that city. It is what L.A. was in 1965—with better Wi-Fi. I met with Mabs. She couldn't help much but rode with me to Ziggy's and to The Dirty Fortune Cookie.

The bar wasn't open until four. The restaurant staff turned over with every college year, if not semester, so no one remembered the girl in the photograph I showed them. But they said most business was done in the evening. Come back later. The Chinese restaurant's busiest time was when the club closed at 2:00 am. Before leaving, I bought Chinese takeout for Mabs and me. We ate it on the picnic tables under the trees at the side of the restaurant.

I went back after dark. They were right about Austin at night. The club was hopping and with the reggae band playing Marley covers, the smell of ganja was strong in the parking lot. I showed Nev's photo to the bartenders and wait staff. The bouncer was the senior employee. He had less than two years employ. My missing person's case was old news here, and everyone was new. I called it quits there and drifted to The Dirty Fortune Cookie.

I showed the photo to the stoners filling takeout orders from a side window facing the street. I told them she might have been with a performer from a couple of years ago, a guy named Jack Frost.

The guy looked at it. "Can I see it?"

I handed Nev's photo to him.

He put his hand over the top part of the photo, covering Nev's chestnut brown hair. He showed it to his partner who had that chronic reek to his clothes. "It's the Ice Maiden, right?"

His friend gave a stoned laugh. "Yeah, man. It is. Just without the shock wig."

"What?" I asked.

"You know, Jack Frost wore this silver spiky wig on stage. Like Quicksilver in the Marvel movies. Then when this chic-kee-do moved in on him, she started wearing one too. Best looking couple ever, I guess. Very hip, but she was only around a couple of times. Him, he got Chinese three times a week for, like, two years running."

"You're sure it's her?"

"Yeah, definitely. Although I must admit I spent more time checking the Ice Maiden's rack and ass than her face."

"Yeah man," agreed the stinky stoner beside him.

I found out the next day that Jack Frost's real name was Turner Best. I got that through the talent agency which had booked Jack Frost into the club. They gave me his agent's name. I called and spoke with her. Turner had quit performing she said, but she was nice enough to give me his contact information. I checked but had no luck. He no longer lived at the address she gave me, and the phone, with an Austin area code, was disconnected.

Before leaving town on the redeye to Vegas and then to L.A., I had one more thought. I stopped by The Dirty Fortune Cookie once more. It was early evening, and the takeout window business was slack. My two dudes were, of course, in the alley burning one.

"Hey, it's you again. Find the Ice Maiden?"

"No, not Jack Frost either. His real name is Turner Best."

"Cool. Want a hit on the spliff?"

I puffed the joint once as a courtesy, thinking it might help garner candid answers.

"You ever see Jack Frost's band play?"

"Sure, they were the thing back in '15 and '16."

"Tell me about them."

"Space music. Think psychedelic stuff crossed with goth posturing. The Cure with Pink Floyd intros."

"No, not the music. About the band. How many members?"

"Oh wow, maybe three or four of them. A guy on drums, a guitarist—Jack played keyboards and sang. Mostly sang."

"Anybody else?"

The other dude spoke for the first time, "The chick on bass. She was fine as wine in the summertime."

"Oh yeah, how could I forget her?" He looked down at the joint I had returned to him. "Oh, that's why." He laughed. "Yeah, the tall chick who played bass."

"She was tall, maybe like 5-9?"

"Probably about right."

"How tall was Jack Frost?"

"Way taller," they both answered. "Maybe six-six."

"That's pretty tall," I said.

"Well, it's Texas," he said. "We grow 'em big and everybody wears boots."

From the airport before boarding, I called Roddy. I told him I thought members of a rock band from Austin called Jack Frost had been involved in the robbery. I told him I knew Nev Martin had a relationship with Turner Best, the lead singer. I did not know the other members' names. He said he would research it. He also said he would conduct a Mambo report on each name. That was our nickname for a report giving us a person's social security number, their credit report, and any financial information associated with the relevant social security number. It was an illegal act, but Roddy did it routinely without leaving a trace. It was helpful having a computer whiz as a partner—ex-partner—in a detective agency.

When I landed in Vegas at 2:00 in the morning, I had an urgent text message to call Roddy.

"What's up?" I asked.

"Me, burning the midnight oil. Got your names and financials, or lack thereof."

"Give it to me."

"Five members in the band—Turner Best you know. The others are Nick Reynolds, lead guitar; Jay Miley, drums; Doreen Lister on bass, and Rob Bonnet listed as manager, lights and tech."

"Terrific. You got addresses?"

"Got everything you want—on Rob Bonnet. He's now an engineer for a record label there in Austin. Getting good reviews. His credit is good. No big deposits. He spends roughly what he makes. Let me give you his phone number."

He did. I wrote it down.

"What about the rest of them?"

"Almost nothing. Not for two years. Not one credit card transaction. No active cell phone records. Nothing for all four band members."

"Three inside the bank with Landaugh, one outside holding Nev hostage?"

"That's what I'm thinking. And now they disappear without an electronic trace."

"You said almost."

"Yeah, there is one thing. Doreen Lister, the bassist, sold a farm outside Sacramento. Received seven hundred grand. Later. She closed the account after transferring the full amount from the local yokel bank to the Royal Bank of the Cayman Islands."

I whistled.

"Yeah, I agree. Think you should rebook and go to Sacramento before you come home?"

"Yeah."

There was not a flight to Sacramento until 6:30 am, but it was already overbooked. I bought a ticket on the next available flight at 10:30 am, then caught a taxi to the Delano Las Vegas. I checked into a spiffy room and slept from three to eight. I rolled out of bed with the alarm, made coffee, took a shower, and called Detective Vega. He was at his desk, but he was grouchy.

"Hey Vega, Clayton Grace here. Got a question for you."

"I'll see if I got an answer."

"You need more coffee, sounds like."

This time, I think, he growled before he spoke. "What do you need?"

"You ever look into Nev Martin's trips to Austin?"

The detective laughed. "You mean the one a full year before the robbery or the one six months before that? I hope you aren't soaking that poor widow for a big wad of cash. I ain't got time for this bullshit."

"I'm not charging her a cent."

"Then you're trying to get in her pants. Well, there's easier ways. And ways that won't break her heart again. You suck, Grace. I thought you said you wouldn't waste my time."

"I take that as a no. You didn't look into her trips to Austin."

"No, and I didn't investigate her father/daughter fishing trip either. I gotta go. I have work to do."

Vega hung up.

I called Linda next.

"Did you find anything out in Austin?"

"It's too early to tell. I'll let you know when I find out anything for sure. I do have some more questions."

"Sure. Whatever you need to know."

"How many times did Nev go to Austin?"

"Twice. A week each time. Fall of her freshman year, then again over spring break that next year."

"And she went on a fishing trip with Landaugh the following year?"

"Yes, and that was strange. I didn't think either of them liked to fish. But they went. Somewhere outside of Sacramento. They sent me photos. I went to see my mom that week. She died last fall after a couple of tough years." Linda paused. "I can send you a photo of Lanny and Nev fishing."

"Yeah, do that. I am headed to Sacramento in a couple of hours."

Linda laughed nervously. "I can't imagine why their fishing trip matters."

"It probably doesn't," I said, reassuring her. "But I am running down every lead. I'll call you when I get back to L.A. this evening."

"Come over when you get back. Whatever time it is. I am so on edge with all this getting stirred up again. I need to see you. Know you're okay."

I agreed to meet her for a late dinner and then ended the call with my heart racing.

~

My next call was to Rob Bonnet, the ex-manager of Jack Frost. He answered on the first ring.

"This is Rob."

"Hi Mr. Bonnet, I'm a private detective, Clayton Grace. I've been hired to find the members of Jack Frost. You managed them until a couple of years ago. Is that correct?"

He laughed through the line. "Yeah, it *would* take a detective to find them these days."

"Why do you say that?"

"Oh, they left town pretty much owing everybody something."

"You know where they went?"

"Los Angeles," Bonnet said, "like all the rest of them. Starstruck. Gonna get the big record contract. L.A.—where good musicians go to die. Have you heard their album?"

My ears perked up. "No," I said.

"Yeah, no one else has either. L.A. is not really a good place to get signed these days. Austin or Nashville are much better, but Turner, he just wouldn't listen to me."

"Then you've had no contact with any of them since when?"

"Thanksgiving time two years ago."

"Thanks."

"Good luck," Bonnet said. "If you find them, tell them they still owe me two grand."

When I landed, Roddy had texted me the name of the realtor who had conducted the sale of the property for Doreen Lister. I laughed when I read the name. Buckminster White-horse was quite a name – and sure enough, his middle name was Nash, I discovered. Buck N. Whitehorse was the man I needed to meet.

He was a friendly cuss, I'll say that.

"Yeah, I handled that sale. Knew the family for forever. Sad story."

"How so?"

"Well, the old man, Elston, that would be Doreen's grand-father. He was a solid citizen. A good farmer. Made something out of that place. About three hundred acres, and only fair soil, but he done made something out of it. 'Course, then he passed."

"And the son? Doreen's father?"

Buck raised an eyebrow. "Elmer, he was a drunk. His wife got the cancer. Up and died. Doreen's older sister died of drugs down to Reno, it was. Doreen was the youngest, but she got out as soon as she could. Think she even ran away a few times before being gone stuck, if you know what I mean."

"Any more family to speak of?" I asked.

"No sir."

"How'd her father die?"

"It was only a matter of time. He ran off the road and kilt himself."

"When was this?"

"Thanksgiving week, two years back."

"Any witnesses?"

"Nah. Nobody with any sense would be out that late. Newspaper carrier found the vehicle down the ridge the next morning. Coroner said he'd been dead for a good bit. Killed on impact. Fractured skull."

"And Doreen decided to sell the farm?"

"Oh yeah, she hated that place. Wanted shut of it. Strange though, she lived in Austin, Texas, but was at a hotel in Sacramento when the sheriff called her about her father's death. She was out here to see me that very afternoon. 'Fore the body was cold, so to speak."

"Anybody with her?"

"Handsome guy. Didn't get his name."

"How long did it take to sell?"

"Oh, it was a seller's market then. I went to her and said I could get her an offer before we had her daddy in the ground if she wanted. But she wanted to hold off a bit. For decorum, I guess. Good manners, I think. Plus, Doreen said she wanted to make improvements to the place before it went on the market. That had me scratching my head.

"Then she called me out a few days later, must have been December 3rd. Doreen and that good-looking feller had rented a caterpillar and leveled the house. Buried it by pulling down the hillside on it."

"Tell me about that. What was the house like?"

"A ramshackle joint by that time. Held together by baling wire and snot. It was a split level with a two-car garage under. All gone now. Got to admit she did improve the property by getting rid of that eyesore."

"Doreen just buried it all?"

"Yeah, gave me a big laugh. Doreen signed papers when I met her out there. Gave me power of attorney. I sold the place the next week. Closed on December 12th, took my commission and deposited the rest into the saving bank in town. All by the books."

"I'm sure. Can you take me to the farm?"

"I don't have too much on the docket. Let me call the new owner, Mick Brown. He should be able to meet us. A hell of a guy."

Mick Brown *was* a hell of a guy. He was only too glad to show me his farm and the improvements he had made to the Lister spread. He had a dandy herd of cattle out there now. Buck was positively perky as he inspected the number of spring calves.

But I had both Mick's and Buck's mouths gaping open when I asked if I could pay to excavate the property. Mick balked, saying he had a sizable number of cattle on it and was worried about their welfare. He didn't want to upset his cute, little calves and their mammas. I told him I would pay to do the digging, pay to fill it back in, and give him a thousand to boot.

Mick said two. I said okay. Buck smiled broadly.

"Why would you want to dig up that ole house? What are you looking for?" Buck asked.

"Bodies," I replied. Now that got Mick and Buck's goat. So much so, Buck offered to buy me lunch to pump me for more info. But I turned him down, telling him I had business to address, and asked him for the best hotel in town.

Then I called Roddy and put him to work. He found a contractor who could complete the dig tomorrow. I called Linda, reluctantly cancelling our late dinner. I avoided telling her I believed I would find the bodies of her husband and daughter in the morning.

Linda knew something was wrong. "Be careful," she said. "You're important to me. More than you know."

I said I would.

The house was under three feet of rich loam soil. It was an easy excavation. Pulling the demolished house apart took a bit more time, but we were successful. We found the bodies inside a beat-up Mini-Cooper under the crushed walls of the garage. It was not quite noon when the excavator gave me the number for the village's coroner. I took the time to call Vega.

I told the detective I found bodies in the demolished home. Vega cursed me for holding out on him. As I was holding the phone away from my ear, listening to Vega's lecture on me fucking up his investigation, the coroner walked up.

I told Vega to clamp it for a second. "What you got?" I asked the woman in the yellow hazmat suit and boots. She lowered her mask. Coroners do not talk fast. They are used to their patients having patience. She wiped her brow and pursed her lips before speaking.

"Two bodies, been there a long time. Probably two years, just like Buck Whitehorse confirms on the home demolition and sale. Matches the timeline of decomposition. Advanced stages of decomposition on both corpses. Identification will take time."

"Man and woman, right? Woman young. Brown hair. Man in his forties, blond?"

The coroner looked at me, confused. "No. These are two young males, maybe twenties. Both with long dark hair. Gunshots to the backs of their heads. One each. Kill shots. Close range."

I realized I still had Vega on the phone. "It's not them," I said.

"What?" Vega said. "What do you mean?"

"Two males, youngish, long hair. It's not Landaugh or Nev."

"Damn you, Grace," Vega started again. I hung up.

After that, the sheriff had lots of questions. I missed the last flight again that night, and I cancelled with Linda again, but didn't tell her about finding the bodies. It wasn't her family, and it would just be too hurtful and complicated over the phone.

I spoke to Roddy from my Sacramento hotel room that evening. I told him what I told the sheriff, the coroner, and later Fernando Vega, that the two dead men were likely Nick Reynolds and Jay Miley, members of a rock band called Jack Frost from Austin, Texas. Doreen Lister, the woman who had sold the house, had played bass for the group. Nev had been in a relationship with the band's lead singer, a man named Turner Best. I told them that was all I knew. And it was.

It was Roddy's turn to whistle. "Look at you, bro. On the case less than a week and you're running rings around Vega. He's got to hate your guts. Man, have you made him look bad."

"I have that knack. Winning friends and influencing people."

"Stop it. You're awesome. And I have news. After you told me that Buck Whitehorse deposited Doreen's share of the farm's proceeds into the local savings bank, I looked to see if anyone had ever accessed that account. I mean, before the transfer. The account was only active for about a week."

"And?"

"Only once. From an IP address at the public library of Boise, Idaho."

"Think that's where they went?"

"Yeah, now I do. Until noon today, I thought maybe the whole band was up there writing killer songs, pun intended, but now it appears that Landaugh and Nev might still be alive."

"With Doreen and Tucker."

"Can I have Double Stockholm Syndrome for $500, Alex?"

I laughed at the absurdity of it. "I've been thinking about that. Was Landaugh the mastermind? I mean, how could have any of the rest of them know about the Christmas bonus extra million in cash at the bank that day? It was only there that one day, once a year. December 1st."

"That would be a good question to ask Linda."

"I will. I need to fly home. Dapper will need food."

"I went up and fed him some burgers."

"Thanks. What are you working on?"

"Searching for home purchases in the Boise area. Out in the boondocks. Compounds, off the gird stuff. I figure they used Doreen's money to reinvest. That way they didn't have to explain two mil in cash. But there's plenty of shady characters in the woods up there."

"Around Boise?" I laughed. "The expression 'shady neighbors' is in the city's promotional relocation description."

"White supremacy discounts," Rod added.

We both laughed. I loved working with this guy.

"Night, bro."

"Give my love to Karen, Gracie, and Jerry."

"Will do." Then Roddy hung up.

I called Linda before I went to sleep. I must have woken her up because her voice was dreamy, like she was coming up from underwater.

"Oh, you," she said. "I was dreaming."

"Good dreams, I hope."

"Oh yes, very good."

"Sorry to wake you up then," I said, regretting taking a

business tack. "Rod had a question and I said I would ask you."

"Okay, when are you coming home?"

"Tomorrow morning early."

"Good, come see me."

"I will."

"What's the question?"

"Would Nev have known that Carson Citizen's Bank was planning to have a million extra dollars on hand December first?"

"Oh, sure," Linda said, suddenly more awake and less sultry. "She worked there as a teller before Landaugh got hurt. When she was sixteen, she worked there for about a year and a half. The bank always hired kids as tellers and to help with data entry during the Christmas rush. The fiberglass plant employees are transients and most of them don't have bank accounts, so the plant has the Christmas money put into checking accounts for them. The employees don't have to utilize the accounts, of course, and most probably just cash the money out, but some get the account, start to save. It's a good thing. Nev put it on her resume."

"Thanks," I said. I hung up, looking forward to the morning. But the conversation made me uneasy. Now I believed Nev Martin told her boyfriend Turner Best about the bank's large cash holding on December first in 2017. They decided to steal it. Lucky for them, they had an inside man—Landaugh Martin, bank guard.

Before I went to sleep, my phone beeped after I received a text message. A text from Linda. I opened it, a photo. A beaming Landaugh and Nev stood before the camera, holding fishing tackle. They looked alive and happy. I hoped they still were, but I wondered. I also wondered who had taken that photo.

At dawn, I was at the Sacramento airport. There was a flight to John Wayne, so I changed my ticket. Landing before eight, I grabbed my bag and Ubered to Linda's home. I arrived in less than thirty minutes. She opened the door wearing what I guessed was only an oversized t-shirt. Her hair was mussed, and there was still sleep in her eyes. She held a coffee cup.

"Good morning, Clay. You must have gotten up early."

I stepped inside and we stood close, her eyes looked up into mine.

"You need coffee?"

"Later.," I said. "You naked under that tee?"

She laughed. "I thought you were a detective. Investigate."

I pulled her into my arms.

"Oh my," she said, in jest, "you must be a detective. You're packing heat."

Much later, I awoke. Linda was out of bed and I could hear kitchen sounds. I rolled out and reattached my prosthesis. Although I am usually self-conscious about people seeing my stump, my leg gone just below my left knee, I hadn't given it a thought until now. Passion is a funny thing.

"There's a robe on the back of the door," Linda called, hearing me banging around.

I found it—a large puffy yellow terrycloth robe with a tasseled belt—definitely my style. I entered the kitchen. She looked at me and laughed.

"Sorry. I gave all Landaugh's clothes to charity."

"It feels less awkward wearing this Big Bird thing than it would have wearing his," I said.

Linda nodded and poured me a fresh cup of coffee. She nodded to the bedroom. "That was nice," she said. "And long overdue."

"Twenty years overdue?" I asked and then regretted it.

She saw my wish to rewind the moment in my eyes and just shrugged. We were saved by the awkwardness by my cell phone's ring. It was the Dragnet theme song, my ring tone for Captain Janelle Jackson.

"Morning, Janelle."

"Hiya, Grace. You sound sleepy. I wake you?"

"Yeah, I just woke up."

"Really?" she said. "I called Roddy and he said you flew back early this morning. I sent a patrol car up to your trailer, but they only found one coyote." She laughed. "Where are you?"

"Didn't say I was sleeping at home."

"Oooo," Janelle purred. "Do tell."

"I think not. What do you need?"

"Detective Vega told me you found a couple of bodies up in Sacramento. Band members of Nev Martin's boyfriend?"

"Yeah. Surprised me. Can't really talk about it right now," I said, looking at Linda.

"Oh, you're with Landaugh's widow? You know, Clayton, I'm a detective too. I figured that out all by myself."

"Why'd you send the black and white up to Topanga?"

"Thought you might 'grace' us with your presence and give us a statement. Detective Vega, who is not your biggest fan, said you've been working on the Carson Citizen's cold case for about a week. We want to know what you uncovered."

"Okay, I can do that. Playing catch up, though. Tomorrow be okay?" I needed to do laundry, feed Dapper, and get some shuteye. But right now, as soon as I could end this call, I planned on making love to Linda again.

"See you tomorrow at 8:00," Captain Janelle Jackson said in her official voice, signing off.

My phone rang again before I even set it down. It was Roddy.

"I found it."

"What?" I asked, not following.

"I found the compound," he said. "I spent last night going through real estate transactions near Boise. I found it."

"Tell me."

"House on fifteen acres, outbuilding with 'cold weather' access sold for $825 thousand. Mr. and Mrs. Larry and Doris Smith purchased the property with seven hundred down and a land contract for the remainder. Paid cash on the down. Wire transfer. Bank not named."

"Buyers' names are close. Price is right."

"Yeah, and that 'cold weather' access? That means

tunnels from the house to the garage, barn, and storage shed. I checked. Landaugh would love that, right?"

"Yeah," I said, looking at Linda who was putting scrambled eggs onto two plates.

"How soon can you be at LAX? I got Vakha Bahaev meeting you."

"Why Vakha? Why LAX?"

"Because Janelle Jackson is a bloodhound, man. Now that there's a murder involved, the FDIC announced a million dollar reward if our assistance leads to the recovery of the balance of the money and the capture of the perpetrators. We have to get there first."

"Gotcha. Who all is going to be there?"

"Whole gang, pretty much," Roddy said. "Penny and RoBo are already in the air. I am bringing the ordnance with me. Driving up. Cold weather gear. Boise's got eight inches of snow on the ground. Rat and Fortune are riding up with me. Taking turns at the wheel. Two Escalades. How soon to LAX?"

"I flew into Orange,"

I could hear the smile over the phone. There was a short pause.

"You got your jeep?"

"No."

"Okay, text me Linda's address. I'll have a car there within the hour. Meet Vakha at your gate in LAX. I'll text the info to you. He'll have your ticket." Another pause. "Get your game face on. Got a million bucks on the line."

Roddy hung up. Linda and I ate breakfast quickly, made love less quickly, and I showered and dressed just in time for the limo' arrival. I neglected to tell her that I was leaving to meet six soldiers of fortune to bring her husband and daughter and their compatriots home dead or alive for a million dollar bounty.

Vakha handed me my ticket with the stern words. "We miss first flight. Now not land until 2:00."

I apologized, but the flight was on time. We landed, retrieved our bags, mine full of dirty laundry, and proceeded to the taxi line outside.

"You not have weapon?"

I looked at the Chechen curiously. "No, no one's supposed to bring guns aboard. I hope you didn't."

Vakha shook his head. "We Uber to gun store."

And we did. Right to Overland Armament at the mall.

Inside, Vakha said to the clerk, "We need two nine-millimeter handguns. I like Beretta 92XI. You have two?"

"The Walthers are $350 less each," I offered.

"You will like the Berettas. Please we take two. Four extra magazines, four hundred rounds. Eight boxes fifty."

The clerk nodded happily at the two thousand dollar purchase. "How will you be paying?" he said to Vakha.

"Oh, I am foreign national. Cannot buy. My friend pay."

Roddy had arranged for a rental Range Rover to be waiting for us. We checked into the Grove Hotel and the young woman behind the counter attempted to make our visit the best Boise could offer.

"Are you here for the Real Estate Convention?"

"No. Just visiting friends," I said.

Vakha smiled.

"How about tickets to the Art Museum? It's right down the street."

"No thanks."

"Dinner reservations?"

"Got plans already made."

She nodded, disappointed. "Oh, there's a note here for you. A man is in the bar. He said for you to stop by." She paused. "No name. That's a bit unusual."

"My friends are pranksters," I said, suddenly glad for the Beretta in my coat pocket.

But no worries. I recognized our visitor right away, although I had not seen him in more than five years. I had last seen him in the Sonoran Desert south of the Mexican Border. He was a drone flying specialist.

"Hello Paz," I said, shaking his hand. "It's been a minute."

The little pudgy man stood from his soda and iPad at the table. "Roddy gave me the particulars. Said you would take me out to the site and let me run my reconnaissance."

I turned. "Vakha Baheav, meet Paz." I paused. "I don't think I ever knew your last name."

"Ruiz," he said, and with a broad grin, he shook the Chechen assassin's hand. Paz looked at me. "It's cold, huh?"

"Twenty."

"Roddy told me he wouldn't be here until the morning.

Gave me your sizes. I bought you both coats and gloves. Do you want to get lunch?"

"Not much daylight left," Vakha said. "Eat after dark."

Paz nodded. We went to his room to get the two North Face coats and gloves. Vakha and I moved our weapons and ammo over to our respective pockets. Then we took the two drones (Paz only needed one but brought a back-up). We commandeered a bellman's cart and loaded them into the Land Rover.

The property in question was twenty-five miles outside of Boise in the Sawtooth National Forest, part of the Boise National Forest, a massive area of 2.2 million acres. We found a black top that got us close to the GPS address in Paz's phone.

"I don't need to be too close to do my thing," Paz said. "I told Roddy I could drive out here myself and just float my boat, get the data you need, and download it before morning, but he insisted you two be my security detail."

I nodded, approving, but wondering why Roddy had not bothered to inform me. I figured me being at Linda's threw him off.

Paz was right. It did not take him long to map the territory of the compound. Single-story ranch. Three outbuildings. Large pond extending on both sides of the drive on the way from the blacktop. The driveway had a bridge over the pond, one lane wide. I knew Landaugh well enough to know we would never be able to drive across that bridge without consequence.

That bottleneck would be Landaugh's and the other's point of attack. We would not be going across it.

An hour later, we reloaded the drone into the vehicle without adventure. After another forty minutes back to the hotel, we ordered room service to be delivered to Paz's room while he worked his magic.

Another hour later, after full bellies, Paz showed me his map. "Here's the house," he said. "Drive comes up. Curves up to the pond. Bridge across it. No visible security for the bridge since it's covered. Cannot help you there, but getting across it looks bad."

"I agree. If we enter by the drive, we'll have to stop before the bridge. Our assault will come from the far side of the pond."

Vakha said, "Makes things more difficult from distance. How far?"

"Seventy yards from good cover across the pond to the house," Paz said.

"Maybe come from the woods behind?"

"Yeah, I don't think so," said Paz. "See my program details ever so slight changes in altitude in the measured landscape. Here we have all the land covered in snow that's three days old, according to that helpful woman at the front desk." Paz looked over his ever-present soda and smiled. "That snow melts at a steady pace in conjunction with the coverage around it. That includes changes to the environment, like a hot security light or snow falling on black pavement. Those alterations to the landscape will cause differences in melting."

"So?" Vakha said. He was more of a blast 'em-and-talk-about-it-later guy.

"So, we have differences in the landscape around the

house. Slight increases in melting in circular formations, ten inches in diameter. Over two hundred of them surrounding the house."

"Mines," I said.

"Yes. From the size, I would guess them to be S-Mines. Bounding Betties."

Vakha looked concerned. "Very bad mines. Can blow off both of your legs."

"Could only get one from me," I said. "But the point is well taken. There will be no attack from the sides or rear."

"There is a two-wheeled path from the barn in the back. Probably for ATVs," Paz said. "We could come in the back, but it looks rough and narrow. Trees to the edge of the path all the way down,"

"Sound bad too," Vakha said.

I agreed with him. "One good thing," I said.

"What?"

"No guard dogs. Can't have them around with a bunch of mines."

Penny and RoBo arrived before midnight. We showed them Paz's map and recon work. They looked over the map, and RoBo began to plan the assault. He was the best at it I had ever known.

Roddy and the crew arrived before morning. They delivered an assault rifle to each of us, all converted from semi to fully automatic. All of us got AR-15s, except for RoBo, who without the use of his left arm which hung in a sling, would be carrying a machine pistol. Penny had two weapons, his second a sniper rifle, a Sako TRG M10, which is the sniper rifle of choice for Canada, France, and Israel. It is made by a Finnish manufacturer, and the Finns are known for their snipers. Bad ass boys, they are.

Roddy shook my hand. "No time like the present, eh? Let's go get a million bucks."

The plan was as follows:

I would drive the front car in. I would slow at the curve and let Penny out. Then I would proceed another hundred yards up the drive, then veer left into the trees well in front of the pond. Fortune would drive the second vehicle, following close behind me. RoBo and Roddy would dump out after Fortune veered right. Fortune, Rat, and the Escalades were all equipped with video cameras recording the event. That was unusual for one of our operations for sure. But today, we were here for the reward. We planned on being Boy Scouts.

Rat and Vakha were on their own, entering behind the compound. Their job was to hike in from the backside of the property. Once they set up shop with a clear field of fire from each side of the ATV trail coming from the barn, we were a go.

Paz, we left at the road, his drone high in the sky, seeing all. He would be able to communicate on personnel movement with us. We all wore coms in our ears. It was a long fifty minutes until we heard from Rat.

"We are in position."

Roddy nodded to me. "Ready?"

"Born ready."

"Paz? Any movement in the compound?"

"Someone walked to the garage and back in the last hour. Woman. From the photos you showed me I would say it was Doreen Lister. Hard to tell from 350 feet up."

RoBo nodded, giving his blessing. We were a go.

We entered the property at high speed. I was in the lead. Penny had a rifle over each shoulder. The sniper rifle had a tripod stand that dangled over my left thigh, nearly interfering with the steering wheel. I hit the brakes and he opened the door and leapt out. Then I hit the gas, racing the half mile to the bridge, a black ribbon of road running through a wooden tunnel. Snow fields extended to the forest beyond, dotted with mature pines. Roddy with RoBo and Fortune followed close behind me. I began to veer left but heard, rather than felt, the first incoming— a round slamming into my passenger side door. Then I went off the road and into the trees. Roddy noted the lead resistance and went into cover a bit sooner than I did. Soon, five of us were out of the vehicles, spreading across the ridge perimeter fifty yards from the pond.

I grabbed the megaphone from the backseat. Turning it on, I called to the house. "Landaugh Martin, this is Clayton Grace, your roommate at the academy. Best man at your wedding. We need to talk."

There was no response, but that included no return fire, so I counted it a win. I spoke again.

"Let's meet on each end of the bridge under a white flag. Truce to talk it out."

It was quiet. Rod spoke into my com. "Maybe he don't wanna talk."

But in a second, a broom handle with a pair of whitey-tighties came out the window of what I thought might be the kitchen over the sink. I laughed. Rod spoke again.

"Paz, you got anything?"

"Nope. Nobody moving outside the house or outbuildings. Remember, though, they can move to the outbuildings through tunnels. I can't see that."

Roddy asked me, "Are you sure you want to step out into the open? They might just be looking for an easy potshot."

I was wearing a Kevlar vest and an additional armored vest and full helmet. "I'll going to try to bring this home without a bunch of lead flying around."

Leaving my AR-15 behind, I stepped from cover and began to slowly march to the bridge. Soon, I saw Landaugh open the front door. Yes, he was indeed alive. Hands free and up, he smiled broadly at me. He strolled toward me. Soon we were on opposite sides of the covered bridge, thirty yards apart. I noted the bridge's roof gave each of us a modicum of safety from riflemen. Landaugh stood just a few feet from the edge of the garage, chert rock wet under his feet.

"Long time," Landaugh said to me.

"Yeah, lot of water under the bridge." I nodded in front of us.

He laughed. "Heard you lost a leg. Spent two years or more on the lam from the Iranians."

I smiled. "I assume your last two years were a lot different."

"Not so much," he said. "On the lam."

There was a pause. Landaugh smiled grimly. "What's your deal here? You here to kill us? Try to find the cash?"

I shook my head. "Haven't you heard? We found the two men you and Doreen killed over in Sacramento. There's a quarter million dollar reward on each of you from the feds for your capture. Came to take you in."

"Figures it would be you. How's Linda?"

"Like you care."

He smiled. "Oh man, she's still got you whipped. Bloom is off the rose for me on that woman. Found me an exciting partner. Wild woman, Doreen. Doris, now."

"Murderers are exciting, I guess."

The man facing me did not speak, so I added, "The need for speed, that adrenaline addiction has not served you very well, has it?"

"Still got both legs."

"It's early," I replied.

Landaugh laughed again, but then pursed his lips. He was processing something. He paused, then spoke. "Any chance you want to make a deal, take some cash, shake hands and go our separate ways?"

"How much?"

"Half a million."

"We take you, we get a million."

"Might die," he said. "Even if you get us, you'll never find the money."

It was my turn to laugh. "I know where the money is, Landaugh. Remember when we lived together, you said if you ever managed to get a big score, you'd hide it in waterproof barrels under water. Put the money in waterproof briefcases inside." I pointed with my chin on each side of the bridge. "The cash is right out there. How much is left?"

He shook his head ruefully. "A million and a half," he said, not denying my naming the location of the cache.

We were interrupted by a second voice—Roddy on the back-up megaphone.

"Hate to bother you two and your LAPD Reunion Party, but I've got a team out here lying in the snow. Landaugh, we've never met, and I could tell you we have a laser site all beady and red on your chest right now, but that seems a little 1980's Mel Gibson. Mel's lost the cool factor for me, so I won't go there. But be sure we do have a sniper out here ready to go. He's willing to invert a nipple for you."

Landaugh laughed. "That must be your partner, Stumpy, right?"

"Yeah, I upgraded partners."

Landaugh shrugged. "I guess I shouldn't have blabbed about my secret cubby hole for the cash. See you in hell, Grace."

Then my old running buddy dropped to his right and rolled. One shot from Penny went high, and then Landaugh was into the garage. I was in no-man's land. But I had planned my first move. I threw myself backward. The shot from Penny's counterpart clanked off my helmet as I dropped, making me see stars. I rolled my ass off the bridge into the water below.

That water *was* cold. Damn skippy, it was scrotum-shrinking cold. Plus, I was wearing body armor and a big ole absorbent snowsuit. Luckily, the frigid waters were only about four feet deep by the bank. I stood awkwardly, hearing rounds slapping the mud two feet above me. The world up there was full of angry bees lacing back and forth between the ridge and the house. I went under the trestle and pulled myself from the water onto the wooden supports. If anything, it was colder out of the water.

I realized as I sat down on the beam and pulled the Beretta out of my pocket that Roddy was calling repeatedly in my com.

"Grace, are you okay? Grace?"

"I'm fine," I said. "Just cold and wet. Did you get Landaugh?"

"No, don't think so."

Just then I heard a roar.

"What was that? I asked.

"Your Escalade. One of the bad guys just lit it up with an RPG. Glad I got the extra insurance from Kayak."

Paz interrupted us. "We got a bogey headed out of the barn on an ATV. Think it's Landaugh. Looks like same clothing and hair color from my bird's eye view."

Roddy ignored me now, knowing I was uninjured. "Rat, Vakha, do your thing."

There was still too much noise coming from the house for me to hear the shots from our two operatives in the back of the house. However, in a minute, Rat spoke over the com.

"I shot out the front wheel. Just wanted to stop him running out on us. But it didn't work out. ATV flipped. Looks like Landaugh caught his hoodie in the rear axle as it went over. Doesn't look good. Vakha is checking it out."

Another minute. We waited. Remember now, Fortune, RoBo, and Penny are jacking a hundred rounds a minute at the house and the bad ladies and Tucker are returning as much in kind. It was a crazy racket. I looked around me. There was no way up the bank without rising into danger. I was stuck here for the duration.

Vakha, spoke bluntly into the com. "Landaugh's dead. Broke neck. Had briefcase strapped to ATV. Lots of money."

I told Roddy to tell the house Landaugh didn't make it out.

He did. "Hey, Nev, Doreen, Tucker. Your boy Landaugh tried to abandon your ass. He came out of the barn in an ATV with a case of cash. He didn't make it. He intended to leave you behind, but he didn't make it. He's dead. Time to end this thing. Come out with your hands up. We guarantee your safety."

Our answers were a profusion of rounds banging the ridge, splattering snow in high arcs in the air.

Roddy spoke over the com. "Well shit."

A word about Bouncing Bettys. They are a particularly terrible landmine. They are the worst of a truly terrible device in general. Designed by the Nazis, they work like this: When a soldier, or a child, senior citizen, or even a cow, steps on the platter sensor, it triggers a propulsion explosion. That is not the killing charge. The first charge simply propels the mine and its payload of shrapnel three feet into the air. Once at full height in its ascent, the mine explodes, spraying a lethal load of metal into anyone near.

The kill zone on a Bounding Betty is about sixty feet. Injury severe enough to put the combatant out of action due to concussion or shrapnel wounds is another forty feet or nearly so. So inside of a one hundred feet circumference is definitely a bad place to be when one of these mines goes off. I know. I lost a leg and Roddy two to a similar device hidden in a bucket in Iraq.

With Landaugh dead, Doreen Lister had nothing left to hang around for. She left the barn headed due west. Her plan was to go directly across the minefield, spraying the path ahead of her with an automatic AR-15 with a drum of 300 rounds. It might have worked, but she didn't do the math. As Doreen reached the minefield, she began rapid fire in front of her, but she was running. If the average person covers fifteen feet a second across rugged terrain, then she needed to be firing 115 feet out in front of her before she reached the minefield. She did not.

Instead, she began firing about fifty feet in front of the front line of mines. Her rounds set off seven mines. It was not pretty. There were two rounds of explosions—the propulsions and then the mines detonating.

Vakha spoke over the com after we heard the explosions over the cacophony of small arms fire back and forth across the pond. "One more down. She die in minefield. Redhead."

A moment later, another massive explosion occurred.

This one blew out the windows on the east end of the house. Soon the structure was engulfed in flames.

RoBo spoke. "Looks like whomever was firing the RPGs missed the window well and shot the grenade into the wall or roof of the house."

I heard Penny laugh.

Then a full magazine went off close to me, coming from a hole cut in the corner of the garage.

Fortune shouted, "Damn, I'm hit."

"I'm coming," Roddy called.

I felt useless, stuck in a culvert.

A moment later, Rod said into the com, "Fortune ain't bad. Has a furrow dug across a bicep. I got the bleeding under control."

A second later, a dirty white towel on the end of a snow shovel emerged from the garage door. I couldn't see it, but I heard Roddy speak.

"We acknowledge your surrender. Come on out."

Roddy said, "RoBo, Penny, secure our prisoner."

A minute later, Roddy was above me. Fortune was with him, looking a bit haggard and in a bit in shock. I scrambled up the muddy bank. Roddy extended one of his massive arms and pulled me up into the drifted snow. I looked at Penny who was securing zip ties to a very pregnant Nev Martin.

Roddy called local law enforcement. I called Captain Janelle Jackson. Neither was happy to hear we had found the four bank robbers and that three of them were dead. I explained that all three had passed by way of misadventure. None had we killed, I insisted.

"Tell it to the feds," Janelle said and hung up.

We found the cash, 1.6 million in briefcases in waterproof barrels in the pond. It was night before the cops were done with us. Nev Martin was in custody. I called Linda. She took all my revelations as a mixed blessing. We ended the call in a strange place, and I got very drunk that night.

AN ANAGRAM FOR GOODBYE

I hadn't spoken to Roddy in the week after our return to L.A. It was Christmas week. I did get down to the New Parker Center to give my statement to Detective Vega in an interview room at the RHD. There were no surprises as we had surrendered the video from the battle to the FBI and the Boise cops. I told Vega the same story I had given the Boise cops and the FBI. The FDIC was processing our reward.

Roddy was incommunicado with me too. He was busy buying presents, family man him. I spent the time with Linda, going to the trailer in Topanga every other day to feed Dapper.

Linda, for her part, was still in a daze. She had spent the last two years wondering if her daughter and husband were dead. Now, she found out they had been involved in the planning of a bank robbery. Her family abandoned her for lovers, criminals, and killers.

At least that was the Justice Department's take. Nev's story was quite different. She insisted she had been kidnapped by Doreen and her henchman. Nev's father, Landaugh Martin, was forced to participate in the robbery or Nev would have been killed.

Doreen Lister and Tucker Best later killed their bandmates and accomplices. Later, they initiated sexual relationships with their captives, Nev and Landaugh. Pure Stockholm Syndrome textbook behavior. Pure bullshit.

It was a little more difficult to explain Nev emptying over three hundred rounds at us during the firefight in Boise. The FBI estimated she fired at least that many rounds after viewing the film footage and investigating the scene. Nev insisted she believed Doreen and Tucket to still be fighting and judging her participation in the defense of the compound. The Justice Department was playing hard ball for now.

However, Nev Martin was a beautiful, white girl, six months pregnant in America. She was cop's daughter. He was dead. She was a good enough actress to cry on cue. I doubted the feds would get a conviction. They would plea it out. I was guessing Nev would raise her own child—at least for most of the kids' life. However, less clear was whether the babe would have a relationship with Grandma Linda.

Linda visited Nev in the federal jail in Los Angeles just once after she provided a great attorney for her daughter. Nev said under no circumstances would Linda ever see her grandchild if she continued to see me. Me or the kid was her attorney's message. I was betting on the kid. I would be odd man out. Once again.

~

Nev would not make bail. Her arraignment was scheduled for the Monday after New Years. The FBI was going for broke at this stage—bank robbery, assault, murder, attempted murder, and so forth. After that, negotiations would begin. Federal courts were speedy, at least compared with California state trials. There would be a trial by the end of February—if indeed it went that far.

I found Nev's case highly unlikely to go to trial. I put the plea deal over at three years. Nev's child would need a home for a couple of years while momma did time. Linda wanted that baby intensely. I had a feeling Nev would agree if I was out of the picture. I planned to bow out for Linda and the child's best interests when the moment arrived. It hadn't. Not yet.

Linda and I spent the week before Christmas riding Landaugh's motorcycles in the Topanga Hills. Up there in the sand and yucca, we didn't wear helmets and buzzed in the wide open, high desert. We slept under the stars on the granite slab overlooking Mulholland. It was she who suggested we take the bikes cross-country, taking a southern path from her home to Florida.

I thought it was a splendid idea. We planned an itinerary, but Linda did not want to lock ourselves into hotel reservations or having to arrive anywhere at a specific time. We ended up just deciding on a route, each packing a bag of clothes, stuffing two paperbacks each in the saddlebags along with sunscreen. I got her a nice leather jacket for Christmas.

Then I got the cycles, an Indian and a small Harley, serviced. We planned to leave on Christmas Eve. I hired a young hippy-looking pot farmer up the road from the trailer to feed Dapper. Fortune, whose arm was on the mend, agreed to check in every few days to make sure the coyote had water. I even spent the last few nights after Linda fell asleep on my laptop, adding old cases to Roddy's and my blog. I thought they would remind him of the good times.

Then it was time to leave.

On Christmas Eve, Linda and I left Topanga at dawn. Dapper stayed in bed in the trailer. We rode down the canyon into the city to North Hollywood and Roddy's house. On the back of my bike, the Indian, I had strapped presents for Roddy, Karen, Gracie, and, of course, Jerry the Monkey. I had purchased Tedeschi/Trucks tickets for that May for Gracie and her mom. For Jerry, I bought a big box vinyl set of the Allman Brothers Fillmore East shows. Newly remastered. I knew it was on his list. For Roddy, I got a bottle of Siembra Azul tequila and a box set of Mozart on compact disk. That tequila brand was famous because the producer played classical music to the agave plants to keep them calm. It's a running joke for Roddy and me, and an expensive bottle of booze. But it will make him laugh.

Linda and I arrived and rolled to a stop in the driveway. Linda blew me a kiss and said, "I'll stay here. You two need a moment."

I rang the bell. Roddy was up, so was Jerry. Rod opened the door for me. The two had been watching a recorded NFL game on the kitchen TV.

Jerry didn't look up from the game. As Roddy reentered

the room with me in tow, the monkey said, "The Broncos are terrible. No quarterback. Bad defense."

I laughed. It surprised him. Jerry looked up and said, "Merry Christmas, Gracer."

I returned the greeting. "Merry Christmas, Jerry."

Roddy poured me a cup of joe. "What's up?"

I handed him the presents in my arms. He thanked me. Jerry poked through the pile to see his name on the box. "Can I open it?"

"Not until tomorrow, little guy," Roddy said to the monkey.

Jerry pouted. The 49ers scored again. Jerry said, "No D. No D at all."

Roddy said, "Yeah, no D. The donkeys suck. But they'll get a good draft pick and rebuild through free agency."

I said, "I can't stay. Linda is outside. Just wanted to drop off the gifts. We're headed east on the bikes. Going to Miami Beach."

Roddy looked out the window. "Get her in here. Jeez, where are your manners, Grace?"

I waved him off. "We want to hit the road. Might stop early in Palm Desert. Oh yeah, I wrote up some old cases. Finally got them edited. I posted them in the blog."

"I saw," Roddy replied. "I'll read them over this week."

"Good times," I said.

He didn't respond.

I handed him an envelope. "Open that."

It was a Christmas card with Santa taking a crap down a chimney. Inside, I had written "D-B-o-o-g-e-y, Love Grace.

Roddy raised an eyebrow. "I don't get it."

"It's an anagram for goodbye."

He nodded, understanding. "For good?"

"Don't know. If Nev gets jail time and Linda has custody of the baby, probably not. Nev has said her child will not be raised by the man who killed her father."

"You didn't kill Landaugh."

"I know. Doesn't really matter. The child does."

Roddy nodded again.

Jerry grabbed the Christmas card, laughing at image of Santa taking a dump down a chimney. He scanned the words. "That not a good anagram, Grace. Boogey got no D."

"Yeah," I said, "but I'll get a good draft pick and rebuild through free agency."

Jerry smiled broadly and gave me a huge grin. "Jerry see what you did there."

We all laughed.

"Give my best to Gracie and Karen." I had to leave. I was starting to blubber.

"Love you, Grace."

"Love you too, Roddy."

Jerry looked up from his iPad. "There are no anagrams for goodbye."

I smiled at him. "I know, little man, I know."

Then Roddy and I hugged. I know there were tears in both of our eyes. I shrugged away his hug and moved to the door. I was leaving my best friend behind to face the open road. But Linda was outside. It was time I took a gamble on a new partner. I was hoping for an inside straight. Maybe in Vegas two nights from now, I will hit one. I closed the door and wiped the tears onto my sleeve before going back to the bikes.

Linda smiled at me, but we didn't speak. We rode. There was a chill in the California air. The sky was sparkling blue. No one else was on the road. Then the two of us felt the wind in our faces as we rolled south without a destination but maybe a future.

HEY RODDY

Here are my additions to our secret blog! These are old cases I wrote up to remind you of how cra-cra the last decade was.

"The Fortune Teller's Fall" was the first one I ever wrote up. Just never got it edited until now.

"Windfalls" got cut in the *Babylon Blues* edit.

Brand New Me was just too long to fit anywhere, but it is one of my favorites.

"Friends with Benefits" and "Fiends with Benefits" were both online as teasers for *Babylon Blues* but have never appeared in print. They are odd fellows with our weirdest all-time clients! The epilogue is because I am bad at ending things.

Best always. Love you, brother, Grace

THE FORTUNETELLER'S FALL

As I entered the office of the Purple Heart Detective Agency, I heard Roddy talking on the phone. "It just goes to show you," he said, "never steal from someone who owes you money." His voice rumbled with a ragged joy as he laughed and hung up.

"What was that all about?" I asked, setting down two cups of coffee on his desk.

"I ran into Rat last night at an after hour's poker joint in North Hollywood.

"Rat? From Iraq? I didn't know he was in L.A." Rat Templeton had been a brother-in-arms with Roddy and me in the big sandbox. Unlike the two of us, he made it back in one piece and the last I had heard was back home in Indiana.

"Yeah, guess the employment opportunities weren't so good in the heartland, so he headed out to tinsel town."

I laughed. "He was in an illegal poker joint in North

Hollywood for the employment opportunities? And," I added, "if you get caught in there you could lose your P.I. license."

Roddy waved me off. "Wrong," he said. "If I *get convicted* after I get caught, then I could lose my license, The latter is not going to happen as long as we have a benefactor in David Welmar. He's too well connected."

I took a drink and said, "Let's not test his largess on small favors. Agreed?"

Roddy nodded. He sat in his wheelchair.

"What's up with Rat? And why the comment of not stealing from someone who owes you?"

Roddy laughed again. "When I rolled in," he said referring to his wheelchair, "Rat was in a high stakes game. I said hello, but he was on a tear—just slaying everyone. But there was some dude there, a high stakes drifter wannabe, and this dude was flush with new twenties, tall stacks, mind you. Anyway, when it got to brass tacks and sweaty balls, Rat didn't have the cash to call Toy Rogers with the leather jacket, ten-gallon hat, and five gallon brain. I decided to stake Rat for a grand. Rat won, aces—three threes against kings and jacks. Toy Rogers was pissed, let me tell you. But I flexed my guns," and Roddy gave me his two gun salute with his massive biceps built from years lifting weights and pushing his chair, "and the dude walked away without another word."

"Rat turned about seven grand on that hand. By the time Rat cashed out, I was in the middle of a faro game, and our favorite corporal got shit-faced at the bar waiting for me. Our boy passed out. Rat was totally out, wads of twenties sticking out of his pockets, head resting against an empty shot glass. Moron."

Roddy rolled away from his desk and went to his jacket and opened it up. "A grand profit for a minute's investment," he smiled. "But back to my story. When I saw Rat conked out at the bar with cash visibly jammed into every pocket—in his jacket, his front shirt pocket, and his jeans, I cashed out, gathered it all and stacked his winnings a little neater. He woke up and had no idea how he got home. Let alone where the cash went."

Roddy smiled. "Remember this is North Hollywood. With Rat passed out at the bar, it was just as likely that someone might go searching for Little Rat as steal his money."

I laughed. "That would be Mouse."

Roddy smirked. "Yikes, does this suddenly sound homophobic?"

"No, not a bit. I think the North Hollywood Chamber of Commerce will want the transcript of our conversation for their web site."

"Right. Anyway, I put Rat's skinny carcass across my lap and rolled him out to the truck. Got him home, tossed his ass in bed, and paid myself out. Put the rest of his cash in his sock drawer. He called just a little bit ago from a taxi on the way to pick up his car. He figured I got him home. He wanted to thank me, make sure I got my money, and wondered if he had any left."

Roddy put his wallet back into his jacket with a grin and snapped the pocket. He rolled back to the desk. I wasn't really used to seeing him in the wheelchair again. Late last year, David Welmar, a politically savvy arms manufacturer, paid for Roddy to get prosthetic legs after we had done the man a friendly turn.

Recently though, Roddy had worn the artificial legs too often and had been running too much in his prosthetic blades. The combination caused rubbing. The rubbing caused blisters and the blisters were now infected. Now under doctor's orders, Roddy was wheelchair bound again while on both antibiotic pills and a topical ointment. Roddy hated that chair, but the infection was bad enough he was following orders. We both knew how to follow orders when called upon, but we hated it.

"How's the ole stumps, Rod?"

"Still a mess, Gracer. Still a damn mess. Doc says they're better and for me to just stay off the legs for another week, but hell, man..." he trailed off.

I tried to take his mind off it. "Want to repo again today? There are luxury models on the list. Easy pickin's." The year was 2008. The country was in freefall recession heading toward depression. The Hollywood hills were full of luxury vehicles that no one was making payments on and full of laid-off movie execs with the cold sweats. The valley was full of car dealerships not getting paid. It made for opportunities for guys willing to pull legally sanctioned heists. We were those guys.

See, private detectives live on divorce. But as it turns out, rich folk tend to not get divorced when the stock market has dropped in half. As Marilyn Monroe sang in *Diamonds are a*

Girl's Best Friend, "It's then that those louses go back to their spouses." So, no divorces, no clients. At least for now. But repo work was filling the gap. We were paid $300 for a new car; $500 for a luxury car; and $1000 for a super. Supers did not show up much. The guy who bought a Maserati did not tend to go bankrupt.

When repoing, we could almost always bring back two cars in the mornings before the lazy bastards woke up. Afternoons were tougher, but after midnight was good for three or four vehicles if we wanted to hump it and work hard. On a good day we could grab six cars and cash in for at least a grand for each of us, but it was dangerous work. People did not like you taking their Mercedes from their driveway—or out of a closed garage (no admission here to B & E—got it, coppers?).

Roddy raised an eyebrow. "Me with no legs means I'll have to drive again (he has hand controls), and let me remind you, you suck at hot-wiring ignitions."

"We got keys that work most times."

"Bullshit," Roddy said, and that's when the lawyer walked in.

Repo work could wait.

His name was Wilkins—Charles Wilkins, Jr. He was stiff as peanut brittle and had an affected touch of an English accent, although he seemed to be an American. I surmised he spent some time in English prep schools. He wore a dark suit, a lemon yellow shirt, and a bow tie with a tiny bit of powdered sugar on it—or cocaine. It was L.A. Telltale signs like that were usually powdered sugar before noon. We spoke briefly and moved from the reception area to my interior office.

We got settled, me behind my desk, the lawyer in the client chair, and Roddy rolled in after starting a fresh pot of coffee. Wilkins settled in with his eyes moving around the office walls without moving his head. What a stiff—I mean literally. His hair, what little there was of it, was slicked straight back. His face was emotionless, his limbs like petrified wood. He took wire-rimmed half-lensed glasses from his suit pocket and put them on. He then opened a banded file he carried under his arm.

"Gentlemen," he said, "I represent Colonel Wilson Boyd Doyle, retired USMC. He is a resident of Maryland and a veteran of the Viet Nam War. He now works in private industry but in a role still related to the military. He is quite wealthy, and if you take the assignment, you will be well compensated. Because of his military background, and with need for private investigators in the Los Angeles area, he has asked me to engage your employ. He picked your agency for its name and your reputation for handling cases, shall we say, of the occult. You will understand once you hear his daughter's choice of profession."

I saw Roddy's mouth move to a minimalist smile, while I could not help but purse my lips in displeasure. Our case with the disappearance and subsequent death of the magician Trevor Baker continued to impact our careers. Roddy saw it as a positive. I was not so sure.

Roddy provided a cup of coffee for Wilkins, topped off

both of our cups and then returned the pot to the outer room. I took a sip.

"I see," I said pensively, "and what does Colonel Doyle need done?"

"His daughter has gone missing. Her name is Caroline. She is unmarried, at least to his knowledge. She left over a year ago and has stayed off the grid, it appears, until just this last week. Here is her picture."

Wilkins handed the photograph to Roddy as he returned. Rod examined it and then passed it to me. The daughter was good looking, a granola hippie type, 30, freckles on her narrow nose and high cheekbones. Her hair was light brown and curly. She wore a summer dress in the shot, and her neckline had white pique lace around the collar. Caroline did not look like the kind to get in trouble.

Roddy said, "What's the background?"

Wilkins shrugged. "I have had few dealings with Colonel Doyle as I am California-based. I am not his regular attorney. However, we have worked together before and I am familiar with his daughter's departure. There was no kidnapping—if that's what you are wondering. No, the young lady simply left a note saying she was leaving, that she wanted to be left to her own devices. She is a fortune teller by choice, and she wants her father out of her life."

Roddy frowned. "Despite the gypsy, crystal ball stuff, it sounds simple enough. I want the same out of my ole man. Hand's off. Why is Doyle hiring us to track her down now? She seems to have made her wishes clear."

Wilkins drew a single page out of his file. "Colonel Doyle

received this letter by U.S. mail yesterday. He sent this scan of the original to me."

He handed the letter to Roddy who read it aloud:

Father,

While I have made it clear that I want nothing more to do with your meddling in my life, I have a chance for an investment that will set me up financially. I know it may seem hypocritical of me to ask you for money, but much of your fortune would have been mother's had she not passed. I believe she would want me secure and would want me to have the funds. If you could find it in your heart, and I know I've accused you of not having one many times, I would like $100,000 delivered in cash to me in California. I do not want to talk to you. We are too different and we are better off in separate worlds.

Please understand that this letter will be my last communication with you either way. If you choose to help me, please have a representative contact me at the following phone number.

It was signed "Caroline" and a California exchange telephone number was printed below the name. I shrugged. ""It seems straightforward. You want us to deliver the funds?"

"There's a complication," Wilkins replied, "Colonel Doyle mobilized quite quickly on the letter and was able to determine through expert examination that the handwriting is not his daughter's. The expert believes it simply a reasonably good attempt at forgery."

"Looks like we have a swindle in the Sunshine State," Roddy said with a low whistle.

"Yes," the lawyer answered, "and we do not know if the daughter is even in the state or if she is aware of the extortion attempt."

We took the case. We had Wilkins sign our standard retainer agreement, which was five grand up front, but Doyle had researched us and offered double our rates. We agreed to get paid double.

The "ransom" money would be available to us at the closest Wells Fargo branch, but we had to provide a proof-of-life via video uploaded to the web directed to Wilkins and thus Caroline's father. And the Colonel had to be satisfied Caroline was safe and in sound mind to authorize the money. I did not think it would play out that way if she had not written the letter.

Roddy and I ran down the number as soon the lawyer left. It was for a burner purchased in Venice along the boardwalk along with two hundred minutes of airtime. No help there.

"We could trace it if we went to the cops," I said.

"Wilkins didn't say not to," said Roddy, "but I don't think Old Man Doyle hired a private firm for us to get the heat involved first thing."

"Agreed. So?"

"We call the number." Rod picked up the letter and with one of our own burner phones—yes, two can play at that game—he dialed the number. A man answered on the second ring.

"Hello?"

Roddy's voice was suddenly sing-songy. He spoke like he had just scored free Dodger tickets. "Hey, whom I talkin [1] to?"

"Who you lookin' for?" I could hear the flat monotone through the tinny speaker.

"Caroline Doyle."

There was a silence. Then a response. "You got the money?"

"You got the girl?"

The response sounded fuzzy. "What? This ain't no kidnapping. Caroline Doyle is fine. She just wants the money from her father and doesn't want to deal with him herself. I'm her, what-you-call-it, her representative."

Roddy grunted. "And what do I call you?"

"Like I said, I'm her representative. Here's the address. Bring the money."

He gave us a Reseda street address and hung up.

I shrugged. "Guess we're going to Reseda."

Roddy was not happy that I had to pull his wheelchair up the steps to the shotgun shack in Reseda, but he was able to lay a jacket across his lap with his monster-sized Desert Eagle .50 caliber handgun underneath. I pounded on the door. A brassy blonde answered the door. She was well past her prime but wore a younger, working girl's attire. She still had the curves, but too many years on the circuit clung to her like mildew. Her eyes showed surprise at Roddy in the wheelchair, but she was still able to smack her gum as she spoke, "We've been expecting ya. Come on in."

A heavy-set man in a white dress shirt, black slacks and two-tone shoes stood in the entry way to the kitchen. His face was hard and eyes narrow. I could see him from the transom of the front door. He had one hand behind his back.

"This will be a short meeting if you don't bring that gun out where we

can all say hi," I said.

Two-tone smirked and brought the hand around slowly. Amazingly, no one had looked at Roddy in the wheelchair— I tell you no suspects a cripple! Roddy's hand was under his jacket and I was sure his weapon was aimed right at the man's chest. He never got a glance from the two standing in the foyer.

The shyster smiled artificially and slid over to the couch. "Okay, we all play nice. Deal?"

"Deal," I said.

Roddy didn't speak and I rolled him into the room. The man set his gun on the coffee table in front of him as he sat.

"You wanna drink?" Brassy asked.

Roddy nodded for the both of us and she poured four short ones. We all tossed them back before anyone spoke. The whiskey was rotgut, and I felt it burn to my toes. Roddy only used his left hand for his shot, leaving his right on his lap inches away from his weapon's grip under the garment.

"You bring the cash?" The man's voice was, amazingly, smoother after the drink. He raised an eyebrow, saying it, noting to us with his eyes that he didn't see a duffel or a briefcase filled with Benjamins. His voice was without inflection or accent.

I was left thinking, "Generic hood, standard issue," but I answered him softly. "We can get it out of the car once we ensure Caroline Doyle is safe and free. But see, we got a problem."

"What problem?" The man leaned a bit forward. He looked at his Glock on the table which now, I'm sure, seemed a long ways away.

"Well, I'm guessing your partner here," I bobbed my head towards Brassy who was refilling our shot glasses, "forged the letter you sent Old Man Doyle. I'm also guessing Caroline doesn't even know about the letter, and I'm guessing you don't intend for her to get any of the money. That makes the both of you party to 'Attempt to Defraud.' That's a deuce in the joint, easy."

Roddy bent over to pick up his shot glass but instead snatched the Glock off the coffee table. The man was slow, slow enough that I realized he had been drinking since our phone call to get some backbone for this meet-and-greet. Roddy used his left hand to reveal the Desert Eagle, a huge gun. Brassy gasped. He moved the Eagle, aiming at the broad's large rack. "Where's the girl?"

Brassy screamed in panic and rage—but not at us. She turned on the couch and slapped Two-tone across the face. "I told you this scheme was a stupid idea. We could have just taken the ten grand reward, but you say the father would go for a hundred. You stupid bastard."

Roddy and I had to laugh. Then I said, "What are you talking about?" As I spoke, I stepped around the short table and put zip ties around both of their wrists, pulling them snug.

Brassy now was full of venom and was eager to give her side. "We found the girl after we saw the reward online." She looked at both Roddy and me with a keen look—and with as much earnestness as she was able to press into duty. "See, Duffus here and me are bounty hunters. We saw the missing person reward posted on this blog. We started looking, thinking hippies always eventually show up here or in San Fran. It took about six months off and on to find her. We knew she was a fortune teller who tended to stay off the grid from the missing person description, but then the two of us got a break.

"See, we were doing work for this Albanian guy who owns the dog track in Echo Park. Anyway, the owner's wife is all about palm reading, tarot cards, all that shit. She even had this photo on her desk at the dog track of her with her medium or whatever she calls her. I recognized the gypsy in the picture right off. It was Caroline Doyle, although she wasn't going by that name. Anyway, I got the old lady to take me out to get my fortune told and it was Caroline for sure.

"Caroline and me even had a conversation about how much we both hated our fathers. We didn't move on the reward right away because the Albanians pay good, but they're plenty scary. And the old dame liked her palm read.

"But right after, we heard the Albanians are all upset at the fortune teller. We figure they don't like her no more, so we're open for a score. We might not have moved on her if she was still joined at the hip with the wife 'cause those Albanian people are mean. But they said they had cut her loose. So Numb-Nuts here and me stole a letter from her mailbox to see what her handwriting looked like, and I wrote her old man asking for money." Brassy paused and then added, "My sister helped me with the grammar."

The blonde blinked in stupidity. "We figured if he could afford ten grand just to track his girl down that he would go for a hundred if he thought she was getting the cash. I never thought we was doing anything illegal."

I knew the last line was a lie but was not sure about the rest.

Roddy looked at me. I could read his mind. These two were not the sharpest knives in the drawer.

I said, "Our client never told us there was a bounty on the daughter. That's a wrinkle we didn't know about. Rod, you keep an eye on these two, and I'll go call and verify the lady's version."

Roddy snorted at my use of the term "lady," but he kept the guns steady. I stepped out onto the porch.

It didn't take long to verify that Wilkins had been a bit choosy about what parts of the story to tell us. Turns out there had been a reward. Turns out that Caroline's departure a year ago had been after years of abuse. On the day she left, it turns out dear old dad had slapped Caroline around more than a little. Since then, it turns out Old Man Doyle had been using private heat to chase his daughter around the country. Turns out he had stalked her day and night until she went underground. Turns out Daddy was a complete nightmare with a couple of settled lawsuits and two additional restraining orders filed by women in the D.C. area. Turns out Colonel Doyle was a dick.

I came back in. "Okay, you two. Your story checks out, but you' re not out of the woods yet. If you give us Caroline's address and we can verify Ms. Doyle's health and happiness, then you walk away without us getting the cops involved, but you forfeit the reward money for your stupidity and for serving us bad whisky."

I took the Glock from Roddy and trained it on Two-tone who was starting to breath a bit easier now that we had suggested cops were off the table. "Roddy, call Rat. Have him come out here and babysit these two entrepreneurs. We need to see Caroline Doyle."

It took Rat an hour to show up. He brought his own hardware and trained it on the two bounty hunters on the couch. We left him with instructions to put a hole in each of Two-tone's loafers if either of them made a move. Then we high-tailed out of there.

Caroline's address was in Rancho Cucamonga, so it took us more than an hour to get there. The address was for the last bungalow of twelve along a lonely ridge close to the Angeles National Forest and directly south of Mount Baldy. A dead-end road led to the house, and a large set of post office boxes stood at the junction of the dirt tracks to the homes on the ridge. Roddy was driving his truck with its hand controls. He stopped at the mailboxes.

"Hey Gracer, remember the Brass Ass back there said they broke into Caroline's mailbox. We should check it out before we go up. See if we can gather any more intel. See if we can figure out why the Albanians have a hard-on about Caroline."

"You're saying those two had a good idea?"

Roddy laughed. "Well, what the hell? It will give you a chance to work on your lock-picking skills."

"Yeah, and to break federal law."

"That's nothing compared to holding two people hostage —which we are technically a party to at this present time."

I nodded. "True."

It took me about five minutes to open the mailbox even though the lock was crude and basic. Roddy would have had it open in a minute tops. I gathered the day's mail in my hands and handed it to my partner as I stepped back into the truck. He flipped through it, then stopped at one billing notice, tore it open and read.

"Hey, Caroline's laptop is out for repair. Here's a notice that it's ready to be picked up. It's at that computer store in the village. I remember seeing it."

"Really? You remember seeing a random business as we came through?"

Roddy smiled. "One, I'm a detective and thus am more observant than most; two, it was next to a donut shop."

We both laughed.

After donuts, Rod convinced me we should take the billing notice back to the store, pay for the computer's repair, and look at Caroline's email before heading up to her residence. No one, believe you me, ever suspects the guy in the wheelchair is up to nefarious stuff. Roddy can get away the most amazing things. Missing two legs is a definite advantage to missing one as far as seeming harmless. Rod went after the computer.

I stayed behind, but moved up the ridge on foot (yes, just one real one) with a set of binoculars with a recording camera built-in with wi-fi function. There wasn't much cover, but I found a place out of sight of the road, hidden with three-foot high chokeberries clustered before the first bunga-low. I sat on the ground and watched the house but didn't see any movement. An old jeep without a ragtop was parked out front. She was home. I could not see the license plate from this angle. I could see there was a flag hanging by a lanyard off the side of the house. It had a crystal ball on it and read "Fortunes" across the bottom of the image. Bingo.

Roddy had the computer from the shop within fifteen minutes, but he was required to use his descrambler as the laptop was password protected. In the meantime, I was forced to move my position as red ants had infiltrated the bushes. I moved up the slope within two houses of Caroline's, staying on the backside of the ridge so none of the neighbors would call the sheriff on me as a peeping tom. After about another ten minutes, Roddy texted me he had hacked the laptop and was examining the contents, especially Caroline's email. I found a second secure position, this time behind a vacant doghouse at the top of the ridge. Just as I got out of sight, a BMW pulled down the rutted road, passing the first eleven residences and stopping at Caroline's bungalow.

I saw the occupants getting out of the sedan—the first was a stringy old broad smoking a cigarette and yack, yack, yacking away. Then coughing—hack, hack, hacking away. The driver exited the vehicle slowly. He was about six feet tall and wore a fringe leather jacket and cowboy hat. He was thin-faced, looking bored and irritated with the old hag. I watched him with the binoculars and turned on the recorder.

I zoomed in as best I could on the two from this distance, turned on the wi-fi, and sent a photo to Roddy.

I texted him, "We've got company."

He called me back just a moment later.

I spoke first. "Did you see the photo I sent you? Caroline has visitors."

"No, didn't look. Bad tidings, Gracer. Caroline's in trouble. She has this client session software on her laptop, like what psychiatrists use. For the last five weeks or so, she's kept notes on each of her customers on the laptop. But she just started using it—she's only had the computer less than two months, and like the Brass Ass said, Ms. Doyle has little experience with technology. She doesn't know squat about computers. She didn't have any virus protection on the laptop at all. Of course, she ended up with more viruses than a whore in Tijuana. Her computer started broadcasting to her email list. And a Mrs. Emil Dzaferi appears to have been Caroline's best customer."

"The wife of the dog track owner."

"Right, and the missus seems to have spilled her guts to Caroline about her husband hiring our two bounty hunters to lace selected dogs' water with a variety of stimulants—speed, coke, meth—they weren't too particular and were experimenting on how best to fix races. Mrs. Dzaferi was concerned with her karma and told Caroline all the particulars."

"Then Caroline wrote it all down and Shazam! Her client session software, via a variety of computer STDs, broadcast it to her entire email list."

"Pretty much," Roddy replied. "I'm on my way. Be there in fifteen."

I watched the house but saw nothing. The jeep and the BMW both sat in the driveway. Everyone was inside.

A minute later, Roddy called back. His voice was urgent.

"I just looked at the photo you sent," he said. "It's the high stakes drifter, the one Rat beat at poker. The stack of twenties he had last night, it was the half down. The half down for a job. He's a hitter. The woman must be Mrs. Dzaferi, the dog track owner's wife. I'll be there as soon as I can. Better get in the house, Grace. Cowboy's gonna kill her."

He hung up, and just then Caroline Doyle exited the back of the bungalow followed by the hitter and Mrs. Dzaferi. The cowboy held a gun on Caroline's back as they marched along the ridge away from the bungalows. I hurried after them, but I was too far back to be much help.

There was no cover on the summit of the ridge if I ran down the path after them. And they were already four hundred years ahead of me. With my prosthesis, I was no runner, but even an Olympic sprinter would never be able to get to the three of them fast enough that Cowboy would not have time to shoot Caroline and then spray lead my direction too. I crept to the edge of the house and examined my options. They were few and far between, I reached for my phone to call Roddy but then felt the lock pick keys and the master car keys I had for repo work in my pocket. I looked at the BMW. I knew that electronic ignition was too complex for me. Maybe Roddy on a good day, but not me. At least not quickly. But with Caroline's Jeep, I had a shot.

I jumped into the driver's seat and started running

through the keys. The first two for the Jeep did not work, but with the third, the jeep fired up like a joint in Jamaica.

I slammed it into gear and spun gravel across the drive as I circled the house. I roared onto the trail, and realizing the element of surprise was already gone, I made my presence even more menacing by firing two rounds high and wide of the three people a quarter of a mile down the trail.

Mrs. Dzaferi ducked for cover and moved off the summit, trying to look invisible. The hitter turned to face me, swinging his gun in my direction and away from Caroline. I must admit the fortuneteller had moxie. Caroline only had a second and she took it. She looked once at me in the Jeep coming down the trail and back to the man who planned to kill her. Then she leapt off into space.

The heels of her feet hit the slope about ten yards down and she pitched forward like a ragdoll into space, hitting another ten yards down on her back, bouncing once and then rolling over twice before coming to a halt in a swirl of dust. I winced as I watched her, but then I had my own worries as bullets began winging my way like angry wasps.

The old hag suddenly decided she had brass ones and stepped back on the ridge directly in my path. I was forced to hit the brakes and slide to a stop. Dirt sprayed forward across the old woman's withered chest. I saw fury in her eyes and she charged at me and the open Jeep.

The old witch pawed at me as I crawled out of the vehicle at the rear. Bullets pelted the front of the vehicle and the windshield shattered. I punched the old lady in the face and Mrs. Dzaferi toppled backwards off the ridge onto her ass.

Blood poured from her nostrils and she cursed like a drill sergeant.

Cowboy started firing again, but not at me. I stared down the sharp incline and saw the girl was crabbing her way down. Caroline was limping badly. I tried to put one in Cowboy's chest and it must have been close because he whirled to fire just one back at me. Then Cowboy turned tail and began to run, digging his boot hills in the slope as he descended toward Caroline.

Suddenly I heard an engine's thunder behind me. I glanced over to see Roddy's truck bounce into space as he steered it around the stalled jeep. The vehicle went airborne right over the top of the old Albanian woman who screamed and raised her arms as if they would save her.

The truck hit its bumper first far down the slope, crunching a fender, and I realized Roddy planned to put his vehicle between Caroline and the hitter. Roddy's tires caught traction after a thump and a thud, and the truck swung wide of the crawling woman, taking the upslope, putting it directly in the line of fire. Never slowing, Roddy held his massive pistol across the space of the truck's cab. He fired once, blowing out his own passenger window.

The bullet ripped a huge chunk of sod from the hillside just beyond Cowboy's head. His eyes went as wide as fried eggs over corned hash. Roddy rocked his truck to a complete halt. His barrel balanced on the hitter's head. I thought I could hear the Desert Eagle cock even from my distance of fifty yards away. Cowboy definitely heard it. And realizing the Eagle meant business, the assassin threw down his gun and threw up his arms.

It was over.

We hid Caroline from her father in a women's shelter where she received medical care for her bruised heels, severely sprained knee, and post-traumatic stress. The people at the shelter to whom we made a generous contribution had seen much worse. We contacted Wilkins, told him we had the girl but refused to tell him where she was stashed. We explained that the father's bounty on Caroline's whereabouts had put her in jeopardy—that in fact, she now had a contract on her life. The D.A. and the feds agreed to put Caroline into the witness relocation program because of the Albanian mob connection. She would eventually have to testify against Mrs. Dzaferi and the Midnight Cowboy, whose real name was Josef Meinach, not exactly Hopalong Cassidy.

Cowboy turned state's evidence, agreeing to testify against the track owner, Mr. Emil Dzaferi, for contracting a killing. Mrs. Dzaferi also cut a deal and ratted on her husband for fixing races, tax evasion, and attempted murder. Ain't love grand?

Rat let the two bounty hunters go with a stern warning that they were too stupid to be blackmailers. They ran, but the feds nabbed them both the next day and charged them with fixing races, doping dogs, and animal cruelty. Last I heard, they were trying to reduce their potential sentences by volunteering to testify against Mrs. Dzaferi.

Roddy experienced a little hearing loss from firing his Desert Eagle inside the cab of his truck, and his doctor at the

V.A. warned him not to use earbuds when listening to rock-n-roll, which Roddy, of course, ignored.

Colonel Doyle paid us off with our ten thousand retainer and the other ten promised in the bounty. We kept four to fix Roddy's truck and Caroline's windshield, gave one to Rat, gave five to the women's shelter and ten to Caroline. Once the feds relocated her, we never heard from her again, except once on the first day back to the office.

Roddy was in before me, reading the mail as I walked in with two cups of coffee. "You know how we joked about how Caroline the fortuneteller never saw it coming?"

"Yeah."

"Well, she wrote us a letter the day before we took the case. Seriously, it is postmarked the day before Wilkens walked in our door. That's freakin' amazing!"

I asked him to read it to me. I sat down on the credenza and listened:

Dear Mr. Grace and Mr. O'Malley,

My name is Caroline Doyle. I am living a quiet life under an assumed name. I am writing to ask you not to work for my father. He is a bad man and is trying to find me. I have realized as I read over my words that even if you decline, there will be others—not everyone in the city of angels can be expected to be one. So even if you do not assist my father, others will stalk me, track me down. I don't know why I should even mail you these words. It is like asking mercy from a bird of prey.

In wishes for solitude,

Caroline Doyle

Roddy looked at me and I said to him, "Bird of prey, eh? The Desert Eagle, right?"

He smiled big. "Yeah, man. The Desert Eagle. And you know what? She got her wish—the Marshall Service, WITSEC—those folks will keep her old man in the dark. Witness relocation is just the ticket. She'll have a new identity. Just won't be able to be a fortuneteller."

"True," I said, "and that's a pity 'cause she seems to have the gift."

WINDFALLS

My first day back at the detective agency felt good. I had been two years on the run, and then beat to a pulp in Turkey. It felt good to be back at a real job—as real as being a private detective is, anyway, so I woke before the sun in my trailer way up above Mulholland and beat traffic into the city. I arrived at dawn. Roddy would not be in for two hours. It gave me time to get settled.

Twenty minutes into setting up shop, Roddy texted me. The text said he had to take Gracie to daycare and would not be in until nine. Two hours and forty minutes from now. Too long to sit. I decided to get in some gym time. With a change of clothes still in the closet—thanks Roddy —I went to see Tony Gut, my trainer. He feigned that he was going to faint upon seeing me. It had been a couple of years. Tony Gut's gym trained boxers. I occasionally hit the heavy bag, but I didn't put on the gloves today. My hands were too damaged from my trouble in Istanbul to dish out any punches today. I just worked on the weights. I completed a light workout and could see Tony raise an eyebrow at how much muscle mass I had lost. I was weak and he could tell. Tony eventually made it over to me and we spoke. We did not talk of my extended absence. The old man smiled, tapped me lightly on the chin with a left jab, and left me be. Then Tony got busy with a young welter weight and I hit the showers. Normalcy felt good. I was ready for routine.

I arrived at the office at a quarter to nine and put on coffee for my partner's arrival. We had no cases and had no scheduled client meetings on the calendar.

Having ordered from Grub Hub on the way, my stomach growled, ready. Even before the coffee brewed, two sandwiches consisting of eggs over easy with cheddar cheese on brioche buns arrived from Eggslut at Grand Central Market. A moment later, Roddy rolled in. He was in his wheelchair, which was not so unusual as you might think. His scar tissue was prone to infection and when his wounds flared up, he could not wear those prosthetic limbs.

Rod smiled coming in the door, mainly for me, but he could also smell the Eggslut bag sitting on his desk. Moments later, he bounced from his ride to his desk. He plopped into his chair, reaching for food. He looked good. Roddy wore a white dress shirt, a retro 50's narrow painted tie, and black compression shorts sewn shut over his stumps which ended halfway to where knees should have been. *The L.A. Times* was soon in his hands, his wraparound glasses down on the tip of his Italian nose. We chatted briefly, but mainly we ate. As he munched, Roddy's wedged his face in the fold of the Arts section.

"What's the good word? How'd Gracie sleep?" I asked with my mouth full.

"Pretty good for a change. Got up about three hungry, but Karen gave her a banana. Then lights out. We were both awake, so got a little late night nooky."

"Kind of TMI for me, Rod."

He laughed, runny yoke in his goatee. "Eggslut breakfast, just what I needed. Yum."

"Anything of note in the news?"

Roddy raised two fingers. "Country's going to hell in a hand basket. First, the sponsor pulled out of the Guggenheim's exhibition for Ed Ruscha. You know him? Good artist —kind of California-punk street art gone uptown. Got an Edward Hopper on acid feel to his stuff. It seems the bank sponsoring his Guggenheim exhibit is under indictment for a bunch of currency violations and won't fork over the money as promised. Show might not happen now. Which major sucks 'cause I already got tickets for Karen and me." He paused. "Oh, yeah, you and Rat are babysitting on March 1st. Save the date."

I nodded, my mouth full of sandwich. I swallowed some coffee, washing down the egg and bun. "Maybe won't need Rat and me if the museum doesn't have the event."

Roddy shrugged, agreeing but not liking it.

I raised my eyebrows. "You raised two fingers a minute ago. What is the second thing wrong with the world this fine morning?"

"Oh yeah, related story in a way. Rico Culpepper, the kid

who tags all his graffiti with the red chili pepper and devil horns?"

"Yeah, I've seen his stuff around town. What about him?"

"There's a story in the paper that none of the local universities with art programs will admit him, even though he's got his GED now. Seems his felony conviction, although committed when he was a minor, is blocking his getting any financial aid or scholarship. Best artist to come along in ten years in a city that couldn't find art if it was the last three letters in' smelly fart.' Rico Culpepper can't get into college 'cause he sold weed to a fed when he was sixteen. The newspaper also mentions his twelve arrests for vandalism."

I shrugged. "You mean his graffiti. They call those twelve arrests, vandalism, defacing public property, etc."

"I call it art," Roddy said with force.

"I think Rico's sale to the feds was about 30 keys, if it matters," I responded, turning to the relevant page in the paper.

"What does the weight matter?" Roddy bitched. "Rico doesn't want to middleman pot for a living. Working for Thiago Reyes is a bad gig. Rico wants to learn to oil paint. And he's got talent."

"And a rap sheet," I chided.

Rod raised an eyebrow. "Whose side you on anyway?"

I looked over the top of the newspaper. "Whose side am I on? You should know by now, it's me and Gracie against the world."

Roddy nodded. "As it should be."

I echoed his line. "As it should be."

"Oh," he said, "I almost forgot. We have a client meeting

tomorrow at eleven. Dude called as I called on the way in. He was at LAX headed to Miami but will be back in the morning. Crocodile Dundee or something."

"What was the name?" I said, cracking up.

"I wrote it down, but it was seriously something like that." He looked down at his phone. "Wendell Dundee. He's the executor for the estate of Thomas Blaire."

"Thomas Blaire, the missing son of Eric Mason Blaire, the dead guy who built all the municipal buildings? The guy who built half of retrofitted Los Angeles?"

"Yeah, the estate wants us to take over the missing person's case. At least I think that is the agenda for the meeting."

I raised my eyebrows. "Didn't the Dudley and Brims Detective Agency have that? They have over a thousand operatives nationally, forty in Southern California alone. Why would the Blaires want us?"

Roddy smiled his monk smile. "After you've failed with the biggest, you usually turn to the best."

I smiled. "There is that."

"Yes," Roddy replied, "there is, isn't there?"

Wendell Dundee, the executor for the estate of Thomas Blaire, was nothing if not prompt. As the second hand was clicking to the top of the hour, he entered. Wendell Dundee looked like his name. He was a prim little man with a neat mustache. He wore a tweed suit and a bow tie. His eyes were animated and intelligent. His face moved with his eyes as he inspected the office from the reception area to my desk. Yes, indeed, Dundee was an encapsulation of what I expected. The only thing disconcerting about him was the size and demeanor of his bodyguard, a huge WWE reject, who frowned on cue as he flexed his way in through the foyer, showing Roddy his biceps. Roddy flexed back, holding a coffee up for display. I watched them preening like two peacocks as Roddy poured the coffee with more arm movement than he'd ever used in pouring java in his life. It made me smile.

With coffee distributed and the wrestler/bodyguard positioned outside the inner sanctum door, I sat behind my desk and Roddy beside Dundee. We went through formal introductions and the meeting began.

"Mr. Dundee," I said, "you called us for an appointment. What service can The Purple Heart Detective Agency provide the Blaire Estate?"

The little man smiled without showing teeth and took a small portfolio from under his arm. He peered at it as he spoke. "Yes, as you may know, I was the Executive Secretary for Eric Mason Blaire for the last twenty years of his life. I was quite young when I first took the position, and I continued after his passing, fulfilling the same role over the last 13 years for his son, Thomas Blaire."

"Who is now missing," Roddy interjected.

"Yes." Dundee cleared his throat. "And you may also know the estate previously engaged the Dudley and Brims Detective Agency to find Thomas. The FBI is also working the case."

I nodded. "Has there been headway?"

Dundee shook his head. "No, neither have made much progress."

"I see," I replied gravely. "Do you suspect foul play?"

Dundee raised an eyebrow and tipped his head to indicate uncertainty. "With so little to go on, we cannot, of course, rule it out. But we have no reason to think that currently. It appears Thomas left of his own accord."

"And you wish us to take on the search?" I asked.

"Yes, the family, the uncles, aunts, and assorted cousins—there are no siblings—as well as me, believe a new set of eyes might be beneficial."

I told him our rates were two thousand a day plus expenses, three days minimum. He smiled, nodding. The Blaires had more than a billion in assets. Dundee accepted our rates as if I asked him for a quarter for a parking meter. I provided the contract. He, in turn, provided a non-disclosure document. Both parties finished their paperwork expeditiously.

"Now that the paperwork is completed, tell us what Dudley and Brims found," Roddy requested, rolling to the other room to refill the coffee mugs, but not bothering to text me any discreet message while out of the room as he often did. My phone rested in the pencil tray of my desk, open only enough for me to see. But Roddy did not utilize our surreptitious method on this occasion.

"Dudley and Brims produced little concrete information which I can relay to you. It is more like they eliminated possibilities for us. Here is what we know. Roughly eight months ago on March 7th, Thomas Blaire, sole inheritor of his father's billion-dollar estate, walked out the door of his

Pacific Palisades home. It was in the hour between four and five am. Security cameras record him leaving of his own volition. He did nothing extraordinary as he departed. However, the security alarms for the exterior doors were turned off. The guards on duty did not, therefore, see him slip out.

"Later, when he was discovered missing by the house staff, I was contacted. We tried to call him, but his cell phone was left on his bedside stand. His wallet was there as well. Now past Thanksgiving, his credit cards have not been used since that March day. We did find that a substantial amount of cash had been misappropriated over the year prior to his disappearance, amounting to almost five thousand a week for a year."

I said, "Wait a second, you're saying he was able to stash five K a week for a year and no one noticed? Who is the accountant in charge of family budgeting?"

Dundee was undaunted. "That, of course, would be my job."

Roddy laughed. "Five grand is a lot of spare change."

Dundee raised an eyebrow but ignored the comment. "I assure you five thousand dollars petty cash a week is not significant in the life of Thomas Blaire. Nonetheless, the monetary situation is more complicated than that. Thomas also left with just over five million dollars' worth of bearer bonds drawn on a Zurich bank. They are liquid, as good as cash."

"So," I said, pondering the money involved, "Thomas Blaire is gone with over five mil in cash. And Dudley and Brims found nothing helpful? Not a single lead?"

"No trace after Thomas went off the security camera

while exiting the house," said Dundee. "Surveillance at all the airlines, bus terminals, even ports of departure for passenger ships and freighters—they all showed nothing. Turnpike cameras at toll stations, nothing. Facial recognition software analysis made no significant matches. No ransom note. No social media usage, no emails, no phone calls. Thomas Blaire just dropped off the grid."

"Do you think he may be dead?" Roddy asked. "Maybe someone convinced him to go out into the night and meet them with the five million in cash? A woman perhaps, or someone who enticed him to go away with them and then killed him and took the money?"

Dundee pondered that for a moment. "Thomas is what I would define technically as bisexual, but he seemed reticent in his sexual affairs. He told me once he was not interested in sex. He lived a life of the mind. He was not romantically involved to my knowledge at the time of his departure. Besides, I've been around him since birth. I don't think a woman could convince him to do such a thing as throwing away his life for her."

"Then a man?" I asked. "Someone who led him astray and then took his life?"

"Perhaps, but I do not think so. Somehow, I must believe he is not dead."

"You really have nothing? Dudley and Brims netted you squat?"

"Nothing we did not have the morning of Thomas' disappearance." Then Dundee changed facial expressions and shifted in his chair, his body language showing he was getting to his big revelation. "Well, one thing."

"And that is?" I asked.

"A note. A goodbye note of sorts."

I laughed. "You held that important bit of intel back quite a while. I take it we passed the initial audition?"

Dundee grinned, discovered. "Yes, I wanted a feel for the two of you before I showed you the note."

Roddy grinned back. I could tell he liked Dundee. "So now we get to see the goodies?"

Dundee smiled again without showing his teeth. "Yes, I will share it with you. Yes, indeed, you passed the audition." The little man stepped out to the guard outside my office door. "Oliver, you may pass Mr. Grace the envelope I gave you."

Roddy grinned. "Hulk does just *look* like an Oliver."

I laughed.

Then Dundee closed the door again and returned. "I'm afraid the note is not helpful. It appears Thomas was not in a good state of mind at the time of his disappearance. No one has been able to make any sense of his words."

Dundee handed me the letter.

Dear Wendell,

You have been a loyal friend to first my father and now to me, so it is with sorrow I write you this note and then shall not see you again. My departure has nothing to do with your service. Please continue to manage the family's financial affairs in my absence. I have every confidence in you.

Although I have not seen my head brought in upon a platter, that does not mean I have not found myself in a wasteland. My biggest foe is my own over-thinking of ... well, of all of it. It would have been better 'twas I was not born a thinking man. But I was, and to paraphrase a famous song-writer, Bernie, I do not enjoy life as one of those who say good morning to the night. To party and carouse. To take my breakfast up each nostril. To not care. To not analyze. To not ponder. I think, however, he might be wrong about where rose trees may grow.

Unfortunately, I do ponder. And my ponderings have found me sorely lacking. Wanting something more out of life. I have found myself surrounded by money and isolated by it. Although schooled in every grace, I live a graceless exis-tence. I find myself without a kindred spirit to share my inter-ests, I find myself in the same straits as E. A.'s imperially slim hero, but without the intestinal fortitude to do the dirty deed and end my boredom.

I began a pattern of thought about a year ago. I decided it was time to be born once more—not Christian born-again, but as a human born-again. This second time around, I would suck of the marrow of life, live anonymously without the buffer of my father's umbrella—not that I begrudge that he kept me from experiencing rain—but life should include rain. Ha, I am a joke. I like the life of an idle rich boy. I am taking enough cash with me to allow me the luxury of a life-time of idle hours. Indeed, I am spoiled enough to know I do not want to live a life of poverty.

Although I know enough to run from this life, I do not know what kind of life I desire. I am too removed from the real stuff to posit a guess on that score—at least until I leave the egg and crawl upon the beach to the sea. Perhaps a sea gull will consume me before I reach the waters of self-knowledge and I will never know the freedom of swimming in the open sea. But I agreed with Henry David, I do not want to live, and not, when I came to die, discover that I had not lived.

Thus, for this last year, I plotted my escape. I decided I would create a new identity. I would hide money—lots of it. I would establish a new home and there I would live a bohemian lifestyle, albeit one with a millionaire pensioners' comforts. I am too weak to strike out on my own without the creature comforts. So, it has taken me a year. It took a year of not smiling when I wanted to bust out in song, such was the glee in planning to escape. To exclaim that I was only months away from parole from this prison you—and my father—so graciously provided for me. Only months away from getting my wings—although I worried that given wings, I would discover myself to be a modern Icarus. Unable to avoid moderation in my flight, I would destroy myself – unable to mitigate my own worst behaviors without your tutelage. However, I had yet to discover what those worse behaviors might be. I had been too timid to act out even one day in my whole life.

So now we have arrived on the fateful day. I will depart and walk to the closest Wal-Mart. I will buy clothes off the rack and leave my fineries and their telltale labels on the dressing room floor. Unlike the great author before me, I have no Charlie to accompany me on my travels, no van, and no dog. In fact, I am more like Dean on the road, though less addled by amphetamines and desire, though I do not intend to crisscross the country. I have one destination already planned. A hidey-hole to start anew. But I, like those on the road before me, will discover America in my own way. I will sing a new song. And in turn, write a new soundtrack to my life.

I don't know if I will return. I may. I may not. Since I do not know of life, I cannot say what life will hold for me. Perhaps I will find the insulation of my father's massive wealth helpful in forging my path. I may find I miss it like the canary misses the cage. For now, I do not have any path except that of escape. Perhaps someday I will again crave this comfortable shell my daddy's money allows me. Not knowing is the thing. I have to experience its absence. Therefore, I shall run like hell to escape it.

Indeed, my plan for the present is to live a life as one of the usual suspects. I shall be Keyser. I will be the Walrus. I will live close enough to have tea with Alice. To see the spot of Eric's sadness. To overlook open fields heavy with fruit, though I cannot imagine I will be able to partake of them most days. I will live within a number. It is that of the lord's charge added to Douglas's answer—though we may never know the question. And if, like me, your life is still too uptight, you may love to get your haircut next door if you should come visit. I know I shall upon my arrival, and I will keep things tidy. You might wish to mail me a present, but no one will because no knows me well enough or cares enough about me (outside of caring about the billion sheets of toilet paper my father acquired and keeps in a bank vault for me). For now, I will dwell alone and although I will live above, I will not be stationery. No, I will be busy with museums, shows, movies, and books. I shall volunteer my time to help others, but this is not really about others. I seek to save myself.

The arts shall consume me with all their fire. And the disguise with beard I wore to disappear in my old life will no longer be needed. I shall have one of my own. I will, truly, hide in plain sight.

Dear Wendell, fret not. I intend to do now what I was born to do. Which is nothing but to drink my wine, but mine shall be poured into a plastic cup (I will live frugally in view of those around me—although I will still indulge in fine wine—and start my day with yoga and conversations with the Mad Hatter. I am not sure if I should seek out a Mona Lisa or a Mona Leo. Perhaps neither. Perhaps the elixir of freedom is all I need. Sex is overrated. Until it is not. Looking for the right candy can be distressing and time-consuming. I would rather have someone who likes the Impressionists and enjoys simple dinners at sunset.

Dear Dundee, do not worry. I am fine and no one has forced me to go. I am sure you will seek me out in all the usual methods. But be aware, just as you have known me all my life, I have known you for the same duration. I have studied you. I know your mindfulness and have planned accordingly. Your usual assumptions and processes will net you nothing. I leave no clues but this. Leave me be. I beseech you to bid me farewell and wish me well (although as I write this missive, I know you will never stop looking). That tenacity is why my father and I depended upon you so. But that very trait will work against you this time. Because truly, I am gone.

Goodbye (at least for now), Thomas.

. . .

There was a moment of finality in the room as I finished reading, and it was quiet for a long minute. Then Roddy said, "Mr. Dundee, is the $100,000 reward for finding Thomas Blaire still in effect? I read about it in the paper. Are Mr. Grace and me eligible?"

Dundee raised an eyebrow. "Yes, although as we now have a working relationship, I should think you would prefer contracted remunerations."

"Could we go the reward route instead of our current agreement?"

Dundee said, "Of course, but then you would receive no monetary benefit except expenses until Thomas is found. You can't have it both ways."

I looked at my partner, seeing a sweet payday of a week of two grand a day go out the window. "Rod," I asked, "what are you thinking?"

Roddy did not speak but took the letter from my hands. He read it again slowly. "Mr. Dundee, do you have that plane you were on yesterday at the ready?"

Dundee looked surprised. "Yes, we always have pilots and crew at the ready."

"Then let's shake hands on the $100,000 reward. We're headed cross country."

"Where?" Dundee asked with surprise in his voice for the first time.

Setting down the letter, Roddy tore up the contract Dundee had just signed. "New York City," he said. "I think I know where Thomas is."

~

Before we left for the airport, Roddy rolled to the other room, grabbed his laptop, and pulled up Google Earth. There he looked at Central Park West, and in a few minutes, he yelled, "Oh yeah. Gotcha. Thomas Blair, we'll be seeing you before the sun rises tomorrow in New York City."

He turned to me. "I got an idea. Where's yesterday's newspaper?"

I went to the recycled bin, removed the crumpled paper, and smoothed it across the glass of the desk. Roddy took it and flipped through the pages. His eyes showed he had found what he was looking for. Roddy tore out the two articles we had discussed the previous day. He nodded at me, confirming. "I'm ready to go. How 'bout you?"

Roddy didn't explain a thing, so Dundee was limited to being a remarkably good sport about flying a private jet across the country for the third straight day, this time with no explanation. A remarkable allowance. Roddy thanked our benefactor and said all would be explained once we had wheels up on the way to the Big Apple.

I knew Roddy's particular secret superpower was at work here, so I let him lead us by wheelchair to the elevator down and out to where Dundee's car and driver were waiting. The limo took us to the private airstrip where we boarded one of the Blair family's jets—this one a Gulfstream G650ER, retail tag of $65 million (I checked it on my phone once we were on board).

After takeoff, the flight crew served drinks and shrimp cocktails. The three of us reclined in captain's chairs around a small conference table at the rear of the plane (Oliver, the bodyguard, stayed at the front by the door as if enemy combatants might intrude at 30,000 feet). Drink in hand, Roddy took the letter and went through it point-by-point so Wendell Dundee and I could finally understand why we were enroute to NYC.

Roddy took a sip of his gin gimlet, half Rose's Lime Juice and half Tanqueray, and spoke. "Okay, I think I can explain it all to you. The letter is just full of cultural references. I don't think Blair is crazy, but he's artistic and an oddball, right? Probably never fit in, right?"

"Like you," I tossed back.

Roddy smiled and nodded. "Birds of a feather flying east."

Dundee nodded, all ears.

Roddy began, "The opening of the letter just expresses his appreciation for you, Mr. Dundee. Paragraph two has dual references toward Blair's mental state. The first is from "Prufrock" by T. S. Eliot. He says he has not had his head brought in upon a platter, a reference to John the Baptist's decapitation. The significance is Blair sees himself as damaged, but not destroyed, not decapitated. Then he mentions "The Wasteland." Both Eliot references would, I suppose, go to Blair's disgust for the current state of our society. The things our culture covets and cherishes, he does not.

"Then in the latter part of the graph, he mentions the name Bernie. He is talking about Bernie Taupin, Elton's John's lyricist. Blair says he is not one of those guys who says, 'Good morning to the night.' That's from the song "Mona Lisa's and Mad Hatters." It is referring to 'sons of bankers, sons of lawyers.' Blair is not like his father—not a business-man. He is an artist, but not like those party-boy, rich guys. Blair says he's an artist, but a level-headed one. For example, he doesn't use cocaine. He also references "rose trees." The line in the song is 'Now I know that rose trees never grown in New York City.' That is where he went."

Dundee leaned back in his chair, amazed.

Roddy smiled and took a drink. He continued. "Thomas finishes the paragraph, saying, in essence, he doesn't have the balls of Edward Arlington Robinson's Richard Cory, to kill himself. Thomas thinks himself to be too much of a wuss. He does like the creature comforts, like good wine."

Dundee raised an eyebrow, leaned forward, and set his coffee cup on the table, and said, "Interesting. Do go on."

Roddy nodded to the steward for another drink and continued. "The third paragraph is straight talk. Blair realizes he wants out. He hates L.A. life. He starts to formulate a plan. He ends it with the famous Thoreau quote about when he came to die, he did not want to discover he had not lived.

"Paragraph four just confirms that Blair wasn't kidnapped. He hid enough money and took the bearer bonds, he admits, to fund his escape. Blair likes the good life, but not the particular one he's stuck in, so he just walked away from it all. In an insane world, a crazy response might be considered sane—that's just me thinking aloud," Roddy laughed.

"Paragraph five is Blair imagining what it would be like to be free of his prison. He references both John Steinbeck's *Travels with Charlie* and Jack Kerouac's *On the Road*. Blair says he is more like Steinbeck than Dean Moriarty, Kerouac's protagonist, because he is not addicted to drugs, sex, or the road. He is more like Steinbeck in that he is searching for a place of his own. He's searching for his own real life—the real America."

Dundee said, "I told you I thought his departure would not be because of a lover."

"Yes, you did," Roddy concurred.

"New York is still enormous. How do we find him?" I asked, smiling at Roddy who loved holding court in this way. He loved explaining what to him was clear as the sky we flew through to two squares who understood none of it. The note to us was an impenetrable code.

"Blair starts telling us where he is in paragraph seven. He says he is within sight of Eric's sadness. That's a reference to Eric Clapton's son and his fall from the window of the Dakota Apartments along Central Park West. You know the song, "Tears in Heaven?" It's about that sorrow. I checked Google Earth, and Alice's Tea Room is just around the corner from the Dakota, facing the park, so that fits too. However, Blair's letter says he won't be able to face the fields most days, so I took that to mean he is not on Central Park West itself, but within sight of the park. The fields he refers to, of course, are Strawberry Fields. That particular part of Central Park is quite close to the entrance by the Dakota.

"As regards to his new identity, Blair gives several clues about that as well," Roddy said, continuing to speak, now drinking a bit more freely on the gin. I could smell the lime on his breath across the table. "Blair says he is one of *The Usual Suspects*. He will be Keyser; he will be the Walrus. I think that's his name. He is living there in New York City along Central Park West as John Soza."

Dundee's mouth dropped open. "You know his alias?"

Roddy smiled. "Kevin Spacey's secret identity in the movie *The Usual Suspects* was that of Keyser Soza. Of course, the Walrus was John as we all know from listening to The Beatles."

"Anything else?"

"Sure, on Google Earth, I found both a shipping/packaging business and a beauty salon on 72nd right by the Dakota—within sight. I think he lives on 72nd. He also says he shall live above and shall not be 'stationery.' The misspelling is not an accident. There is a stationery store at 124 72nd Avenue. John Soza probably lives above it."

Dundee laughed aloud. "Extraordinary."

I joined in the laughter and winked at my partner. "Kudos, bro."

Roddy smiled. "Want to know his apartment number?"

Dundee looked at him in amazement. "You know it? Dudley and Brims had the case for eight months and never saw any of this in the note. Are you sure of your speculations?"

Roddy nodded. "Yeah, fairly sure. The clues about the address are concrete. The address of his apartment is the lord's charge added to Douglas' answer. That is Alfred Lord Tennyson and Douglas Adams, two disparate authors certainly, but both known for numbers. Tennyson wrote 'Into the shadow of death rode the 600.' He was referring to the charge of the Light Brigade. And Douglas Adam's answer to the meaning of life was 42, but in *Hitchhiker's Guide to the Galaxy*, nobody could remember what the question was."

I smiled and asked, "So Thomas Blair is living incognito as John Soza at 124 72nd Ave in apartment 642? Thomas is hiding in plain sight, having told us where he was, but figuring correctly until now that no one was in tune enough with what was important to him to track him down?"

Roddy smiled. "Yep, think so. Blair is also bald with a long beard. A common urban hipster look. He wears glasses now too."

Dundee smiled and asked for the steward to put Jameson Irish Whisky in his coffee. I agreed. "Rod, I think you've nailed this one. We may be $100,000 richer by nightfall."

Dundee sipped his whisky-laced coffee. "I hope and pray you have figured out this whole mess, Mr. O'Malley. I have my fingers crossed."

Roddy finished his second drink with a smack of his lips. "And your checkbook will be at the ready?"

"Indeed."

Four hours later, we arrived at a private airfield in New Jersey and took the Holland Tunnel into the city. Within an hour of landing, now at exactly 11:00 pm eastern, the limo stopped in front of the address Roddy gave the driver. We opened the door adjacent to the stationery store and entered the apartment building's lobby. There in the hallway, we peered at the names on the mailboxes. The name on the mailbox for 642 was not John Soza.

~

It was Kevin Johns. Roddy laughed. "Close enough. Still Kevin Spacey and John Lennon."

We rang the bell. A male voice answered with a "Who's there?"

Roddy replied, "Wine delivery for you, Mr. Johns." The buzzer did its thing, and we were able to enter the lobby and take the elevator up to the sixth floor. I rang the bell and when the door opened a bit, a bald man with a long salt and pepper beard registered extreme surprise at seeing Wendell Dundee's face.

Roddy smiled from his wheelchair and said, "Dr. Livingstone, I presume?"

~

I must give Thomas Blair some credit. After the initial shock of seeing Dundee, his faithful servant, at his door, he grinned broadly and asked us in. He and Dundee hugged. Obviously, there was deep affection between the two men.

Blair said, "As you might have imagined, I was not expecting guests. But I do have coffee on. Would you like a cup?"

Dundee slapped Roddy on the shoulder. "No, Thomas, we switched to alcohol about two hours ago." Then he introduced the two of us to Blair and explained how Roddy decoded the note.

Blair listened, enraptured by the explanation of how Dudley and Brims failed to decipher the note in a year and how Roddy did it in ten minutes. After Dundee's retelling, Blair laughed and seemed genuinely happy. There was no regret in having his new life revealed, his hideaway desecrated. At least at first. But within five minutes, concern showed on his bald and bearded face.

"Wendell, I have to say it is a joy to see you, but what has changed? Why should I go back? Why should I get on that jet with you three, despite your diligence in finding me? I will have returned to the same cage. The same rut. The same bullshit as before."

Dundee looked flummoxed, but Roddy rolled close and removed from his pocket the two clippings he'd taken from the newspaper earlier. "Mr. Dundee, can I give it a go on that question?"

Dundee was putty in Roddy's hands at this stage, so he gave my partner the floor. My partner wowed us all again.

Roddy handed the two clippings to Thomas Blair to read. After he had finished, Roddy said, "Mr. Blair, you're needed in Los Angeles now. You're right. It is a city of shallowness. The performances that pass for art in that town would be considered passed gas in this city. But you're a billionaire— and more importantly, a billionaire with taste. You understand the importance of art. You understand what good art is."

Blair raised his eyebrows. "You are too kind, Mr. O'Malley. But what do the two clippings have to do with me?"

Roddy said, "The first is about a bank's default causing the Ed Ruscha exhibit at the Guggenheim to be cancelled. You have the financing to fix that." Roddy snapped his fingers.

"The second article is about a young street artist, a new generation's Ed Ruscha, named Rico Culpepper. He's got the talent, but unfortunately, he's also got the rap sheet. He cannot get into any school worth its oil paint because of his prior drug convictions. But you have the money to fund a scholarship or even endow a professorship at USC—but you could tie a caveat onto the funds."

Blair smiled. "That the art department receiving the funds provide a full scholarship to Rico Culpepper."

Roddy smiled. "Exactly."

Blair said tentatively, "I would have to meet him."

Dundee stood. "I have a jet waiting to facilitate just that. The limo outside can deliver us straight onto the runway."

Blair nodded. "Okay, I'll do it. I'll go back." He paused. "I'm not saying I'll stay out west, but I'll go back for these two projects. For Ed Ruscha. For Rico Culpepper. And for the endowment of a professorship in modern art at USC or UCLA or somewhere."

The billionaire stood and we readied to go. He looked at Dundee. "You'll have to do something for me."

Dundee nodded. "Anything. You know that. What?"

"Turn off the coffee. I need to go pack a few things."

On the four-hour ride back, we left Dundee and Blair at the conference table at the rear of the plane. They looked as if they had a lot of catching up to do. Roddy and I settled in two reclining seats in front of a dividing wall on the Gulfstream. We were both drinking tequila at this stage and were soon drunk. Both of us were in high spirits. We had just scored a $100,000 reward – and a $5,000 a year consulting contract to keep Dundee up to snuff with what might be important to Blair in the future. It had been a long, but excellent day.

It was nearly 2:00 am east coast time upon departure. We would arrive at 4:00 am in Ontario, California, about 40 minutes by car east of downtown, near San Bernardino. When we arrived, it will have been just 22 hours since I left my Airstream trailer in the foothills behind. Damn, that seemed a long time ago. I have to say if every day as a detective could be like this one, then I would love being back at the Purple Heart Detective Agency. I knew, though, that wasn't true.

Roddy read my mind. He saw my furrowed brow. "You're thinking it is all downhill from here?"

I frowned. "Sorry to be a pessimist. We don't have many cases like this one. Mostly, people find us in the worst way. And mostly the worst kind of people."

"True, brother, true," Roddy replied. "People living in sunshine and drinking lemonade don't need what we do."

"True, brother, true," I said, agreeing with him.

"We wade into the shit so they don't have to."

I nodded.

Rod handed me another shot of tequila. "We do what we do so they can have a day like this again. When they believe they never will again."

I shook my head. "I just don't know if I'm able to spend my life wading through shit again. The last two years changed me. Damaged me in ways I can't explain."

"You don't need to," Roddy said. "Now drink up. And

remember that when I get my stilts back on that I'll walk through the deep shit for the both of us. That way the shit won't touch either of us."

He downed his shot. "Deal?"

I shrugged. It was hard to argue with this man. "Deal," I said, uncertainly.

Roddy smiled. "Now hit your tequila. I'm gonna call Karen and tell her about the hundred grand."

A BRAND NEW ME

He had predator eyes. Dangerous eyes that blinked laconically as they scrutinized me. He didn't speak after we shook hands and I waved him into my office. We walked side-by-side from the lobby to my office. I could hear the morning traffic on Figueroa below us, L.A. commuters arriving late to work. I studied him as he studied me. I watched those eyes take inventory of every-thing in the room. His darting eyes had thick, hooded lids as they danced, but his wide, tan face was impassive. His eyes didn't fit. They were in direct contrast to the rest of him.

He had that downtown uptight asshole businessman look down pat, except for the eyes, and unfortunately for him, they were the feature everyone would immediately notice and remember. They were animalistic green running to a jaundiced yellow. Those eyes revealed a malignance that the rest of him could not hide. They were an uncivilized vestige on an otherwise normal visage. Like noticing a panther's eyes peering out of your rose garden, a place that seemed tame a moment ago. The Brooks Brothers suit wasn't fooling anyone.

Roddy, my partner, arrived through the front door just as the client and I left the foyer. I sat behind the desk; the client sat facing me. Roddy, dressed in jeans, white Dodgers tee, and a blue blazer, waved a hello from the doorway. He attended to the coffeemaker on the credenza behind his desk in the lobby. He poured each of us a cup and entered the office on his mechanical legs. After handing the steaming mugs to both of us, my partner sat, reached out, and shook the man's hand.

"Roddy O'Malley," he said.

"Calvin Grabber."

I noticed the man's grip was tight on Roddy's hand. I almost grinned. No one in their right mind would try to out squeeze Roddy in a handshake. My partner surreptitiously gave me a raised eyebrow and a micro-grin. Roddy withdrew his hand rather than start a grip contest with a client.

Calvin Grabber's build was big, but not as massive as Roddy's. Then again nearly no one's was. My partner's upper body might give professional athletes pause, but the man who sat in front of me, now taking a sip of coffee, would be a handful. I put him at not quite 40, perhaps 6-1, with a thin waist but full shoulders. I get paid to notice details. I noticed this man had uncommonly thick wrists and a thick neck. His narrowed hips and legs were in contrast to arms that when flexed, tightened the sleeves of his expensive suitcoat. I would say we were in the presence of a man who lifted free weights. Stretched over his thick left wrist, his watch was thin and expensive. His cleft chin was set and his jaw locked in this awkward moment of silence, like we were playing chicken on who would speak first. I hoped we wouldn't have to play the staring game too.

Grabber seemed used to getting his way and he was used to order. I gauged his yellow-tinged eyes and his flat top haircut again, thinking he might be ex-military like us. Finally, he raised his hands, tipping them outward like "What's the hold-up?"

I blinked, wondering if I had misread his silence as a power ploy when it was instead a tacit insistence on a protocol he believed was to be followed in these kinds of matters—whatever matter these kind were.

"How can we help you, ah, Mr. *Gra*ber? I said in my best client friendly tone, messing with his name on purpose for no reason I could enunciate.

"No," he corrected, "it's Grabber. Calvin Grabber. Two B's. Common mistake."

I nodded, trying again. "Okay, Mr. Grabber, how can the Purple Heart Detective Agency help you?"

"I need you to find my wife and daughter. They've taken off."

I nodded again. Roddy leaned in and interjected, "When you say took off, you mean your wife took your daughter of her own volition? Your wife's, I mean. Your wife bugged out with your little girl?"

"Yes, so far as I know," Grabber said, moving his chin up and down in a barely perceptible nod. "On her own volition as you call it. She left me and took my ten-year-old with her. We'd had fights, fights about money. My wife's mother just died and left her a healthy sum. We disagreed about how to handle it properly."

"I see," I said. "If I may ask, how much?"

"Nearly a half million after taxes," he responded, "and it cleared probate two months ago. But before it did, she opened her own account at a different bank. I'm on the Board of Trustees at Herold's Financial in Burbank. Own my own financial investment business. Very solid. But she opened another account unbeknownst to me. Had the money sent there." He looked down and saw the coffee cup in his hand. Almost startled, he acknowledged it with a sip. "Without my prior knowledge," he added.

"Without your prior knowledge," I repeated, taking stock. I likewise took a sip, letting the steam go past my nose. "Maybe not an easy thing to see your wife do, but it is certainly within her legal claim, I would suppose."

"Embarrassing, yes." He nodded, but his eyes flared a bit, illuminating the yellow in them. He would be a bad poker player. "Yes, within her rights, but leaving with not a word and taking our daughter is not." He looked at the both of us as if his head was on a swivel back and forth. "Not within her rights." His eyes lit yellow with animation.

"And you want us to find them?" Roddy asked. My partner stood and pointed to his cup. "Heat up, anyone?"

Grabber and I both shook our heads no. Roddy strolled out of the office to the reception area back to the coffee machine. However, he was not after coffee; he was sending me a text. We had done this maneuver before. I peeked down at my phone which lay visible only to me in my barely open center drawer. I gazed down. "Creep" was the one-word message. I nodded slightly as Roddy reentered the room.

Roddy said, "Here's the deal, Mr. Grabber. We don't do domestic work these days. What brought you to us? There are lots of firms in Los Angeles that specialize in, what shall we call it? Family disruption investigation."

Grabber turned in his chair to address Rod. He set his mug on my desk and gripped the arms of his chair. The leather stretched tight under his powerful fingers. "I read about you guys. The detectives with only one leg between the two of you. How you're willing to bend the rules for a client here and there, but you're discrete. Client friendly in the extreme."

"We don't break the law, Mr. Grabber," I said.

He smiled, cocking one eyebrow in the air. "That's not how I heard it. But okay. I don't need you to break any laws. I just want the two of them found. I need to know they're okay. I want my daughter back at home."

"And your wife?" I asked.

Grabber's eyes blazed a citrine blond fire. Poison leaked into his words without his wanting it to. "If *she* wants to come home, she's welcome. It's her home too."

"How long they been gone?"

"A month," he paused, "or so."

Neither Roddy nor I spoke, but we exchanged looks. A month? Or so? They had been missing for a month? Mr. Grabber could read our faces. "Before you judge me, hear me out. Candace, my wife, deceived me. They were to have gone on a mission-trip to Utah. To help at a bible camp on an Indian Reservation. I got postcards from one or the other of them every day." He brought out the cards and passed them to us with a photo of the wife and daughter. "Then on the day of their expected return, I went to the church to pick them up to find that my wife had cancelled going at the last moment. Didn't give the sponsors any reason but paid for their stay anyway. They'd run away four weeks before I knew they were missing. Must have had someone help them mail the cards to me. The postmarks are all from Utah." I wondered if the man's fingers were going to tear into my chair's leather. His grip finally loosened, but only a bit. I could see his hands tremble with anger.

Roddy leaned his head back as he sat down beside Grabber once more. As the man turned his eyes back to me, Roddy raised his brows and mouthed "Wow." Only I saw it.

I said, "Tell you what, Mr. Grabber. We can do this much. We'll find 'em. Make sure they're okay, but I don't think we're telling you where they are. That'll be up to your wife if she chooses to let you know. We'd do that much."

He stared at me. Red tint started to run up his neck. "That's not..."

I interrupted him. "We'll find them and talk to them. Make sure they are okay. Tell them you are worried. That you want your daughter back home. If you want to go as far as to file a missing person's report, then if we find them, we would be compelled to tell the police where they are. You would then find out your family's location through the cops. But we're not going to bloodhound your wife and daughter for you. We won't drag them forcibly back home for you. That would be against the law. And we're not going to bring you to them to allow you to drag them home by force either."

Grabber's face was red. His eyes bore into me with enmity.

"Otherwise," I added, "you'll need to find another firm." His face stayed red, his eyes yellow, but he nodded and agreed to the terms. He forced a smile, but the rage in him was so close to boil the room felt noticeably hotter.

Roddy leaned toward Grabber, putting his one hand on my desk. "It's a thousand a day, three days minimum. Plus, expenses. Need you to fill out the standard contract—Grace, give him one—and we'll need a retainer as well. At least a grand up front."

Grabber squinted at Roddy with narrowed eyes. He removed a folded cashier's check for ten thousand dollars from his suit's vest pocket. He smoothed the crease with diligence, placed it on the desk next to his coffee cup and said in a harsh, almost wolfish whisper, "No police. You just find 'em. Report back only to me. We clear on that?" His eyes moved from Roddy to me.

I nodded.

"Where's that contract?"

I opened the side drawer and handed him a single sheet of paper.

When Grabber had gone, Roddy laughed aloud. "What a dildo, eh?"

I looked back at him. "Actually, I thought he was a little scary." I peered down at the client's two photographs before me, one of the wife, the other of the daughter. I picked up the wife's image.

Candace Grabber was a milquetoast of a woman, mousy blonde hair cut shoulder length with bangs, the rest behind her ears. Her chin was quite weak and ruined her looks. In the photo, she tucked her chin down toward her chest like she was trying to hide her miserable jawline, but instead it made her upper teeth jut forward, and she frowned in the photo in a failed attempt to hide those choppers. She was a small breasted woman with a flat stomach and narrow hips. Her clothes were Southern California Catholic. Loose and conservative. Her eyes were, like her husband's, her most interesting feature. They were like a wren's. Birdlike and inquisitive. Secretive.

I wondered how secretive. After all, she had gone off the grid with half a million bucks. That kind of dough could create the need for secrets. It could also facilitate hiding quite well.

I said, "Hubby said before he left his wife only goes to church on Wednesday and Sunday, to Von's Groceries on Saturday morning, and to the rectory for lunches on Fridays. No known associates other than church ladies."

Roddy examined the little girl's photo. "Sherri Grabber, age ten," he said. "Daddio says she's gonna be in fourth grade. Smart and highly, fervently, religious. Goes to the local Catholic parochial school. Her father, as you heard, says she's never had a girl from school to their home and to his knowledge has not been to a sleep-over. I'm guessing she's not popular with her classmates."

"Dysfunctional parents are such a drag," I opined. "How you want to break things up?"

"You take the school, the church, the rectory. I'll take the house, the computers, the phones. Interview Mr. Sunshine again."

"Okay," I said. "You think mom and daughter are long gone?"

Rod laughed. "Yeah, finding 'em's a million to one shot."

"Nah," I said, "half a million."

That afternoon, we split up and I headed to the rectory first, then the church. The nuns were not much help. The priests less. The former assured me Mrs. Grabber was a pious woman given to contemplation, solitude, and prayer. The priests seemed more aware Mr. Grabber was good for a tithe on a large income each year and gave even more during the season of Lent. The good fathers had no ill words to say about the family. I found one priest, Father Bregoli, outside the living quarters of the clergy as he knelt in a tomato garden on the back lawn. He casually wore a white tee and dark gray trousers and I questioned him as he weeded, crawling from row to row. After he gave me nothing to go on, I asked him, "What about in the confessional? Anything that might indicate Mrs. Grabber might suddenly take a powder? Make a run for it? Anything about the husband that might make her want to get away?"

Father Bregoli tugged a blood red, beef steak tomato from the vine, looking up at me in the bright Southern California sun. "The confessional is a place where secrets are safe. I am sworn to silence. The penitent's confession is sacrosanct. It is part of the sacrament. Did you not know that?"

"Yeah," I said, "I was raised in the Church but no longer attend. I know those confessions are secret, but we might be talking about saving a woman's life. And her daughter's. There is a child to consider."

"We are all children in the eyes of the Lord. How long since you last confessed your sins, Mr. err? I'm sorry. I forgot your name."

"Grace."

He raised an eyebrow as he raised from all fours to his knees. "Grace, eh? Remember the meaning of your name. His grace is necessary for your salvation. How long since you were in confession, Mr. Grace?"

"Too long, but I'm afraid it's not in the cards for today. I've got a missing woman and girl to find," I countered, begging off.

The priest shook his head. "I cannot help you in your search. I know nothing that would aid your finding them." And then the priest tossed the sticky tomato to me, his eye squinting into the brightness of the day. "Churches do not run on faith alone. Mr. Grabber is a generous parishioner. You don't get blood from a turnip."

I tossed the tomato, which had ruptured, back to him, juice staining my sleeve. "Our occupations of saving souls and saving lives should not be confused by the money to be made in the process," I said and walked away not waiting for a reaction.

The rest of the day was a washout. No news and no one

told me anything helpful. Later while reviewing my notes, I decided the only person who might know more than she was saying was the receptionist at the church. I interviewed her in front of a priest and two of the nuns who did clerical work there. She followed their lead and clammed up. That was a tactical mistake on my part, and I would follow up with her again. Afterwards I called Roddy. He was just on the way home.

"How'd it go? You speak to Grabber again?"

"Yeah," Rod laughed, "went to the Grabber residence. Bel Air address, but not so as you would know it. Bel Air by zip code only. A 1960's bi-level—big and outdated. Seems to have been in the family forever. Furniture is strictly Grandma heirloom—if your granny was Liberace. And listen to this, Grabber, that sick fuck, had a key stroke recording device on the home desktop to keep tabs on what websites his wife visited and what emails she received."

"And?"

"No smoking gun. He showed me the report. Nothing to see. She had only restricted access to the internet. Grabber locked his office when he went to work. Even during the evenings and weekends when Candace did have access, there wasn't anything interesting in her searches. Maybe the wife knew she was being spied on with the keystroke device. There is one thing of note. During approved hours of usage, she visited a non-profit called A Brand New Me a couple of times. It's a place that caters to women fallen upon tough times. Gets them work clothes when they are planning to get back into the work force, helps them learn to interview for employment. That sort of thing."

I pondered his comment. "Hmm, now that you mention it, I think the receptionist at the church was trying damn hard not to look at a poster for that place on the church office bulletin board. We may have ourselves a lead. Shall we head down there tomorrow morning?"

"Yeah, wanna meet me in the morning at Malibu Farm Pier Café?"

I said, "Sure, you go early and get a table."

The next morning after a delicious breakfast, we pulled into the parking lot of a Brand New Me. Roddy removed a soft-sided messenger bag out from under the seat. He slipped a device from the flap and set it on the seat.

"What's that?" I asked.

"It's called a Stingray," Roddy replied, "at least in FBI lingo, it's called that."

"And it does what?"

"It's a fake cell phone tower. Creates an extra strong beacon to cell phones in the area, so strong it draws them in to this particular beacon. More so than a typical triangulated signal."

"And then?" I asked. Roddy making me beg for more of his techie talk.

"Then any cell phone in the direct vicinity will send its signal through my fake beacon. The call will still go through, but my Stingray will record all connections made. Phone number to phone number."

I nodded. "Does it record the conversation?"

Roddy shook his head. "The FBI version does. Mine is not sophisticated enough to do that. But it does let us know who calls who. We can see if someone inside A Brand New Me makes a call after we leave."

"Ah," I said, getting it. "We'll see who's next up the food chain. Maybe someone will call Candace Grabber after we leave."

Roddy nodded. "If someone inside there," he pointed with his chin to the front door, "knows anything about the Grabber's disappearance and calls a co-conspirator, we'll know. Otherwise, we just see where they're ordering takeout."

"And if the guilty party uses a landline?"

"We're screwed."

A Brand New Me was at the end of a strip mall full of dentists, dermatologists, and dry cleaners. It looked a little run-down-at-the-heels, but the receptionist was friendly enough, and within minutes she showed us into an office where the lead counselor for the organization offered us coffee from one of those K-Cup machines that squeezes out one java at a time. Mine tasted of hard water and hazelnut. I explained our mission to find both Mrs. Candace Grabber and her daughter, Sherri. The counselor nodded with concern.

"I know Candace Grabber," said the head counselor, a Ms. Sandy Jenkins. She was a dishwater blonde of about thirty-five, slim and put together, tiny tits, no bra, showing off a little bit. I liked her at first handshake, but she wasn't helpful. She was a true believer, it seemed, in whatever she believed. Friendly, lots of smiles, but no go on info. But she did throw us a bone at the end of our questions.

"I'm sorry I can't help you find Mrs. Grabber. She's a good person. Candace was a volunteer here."

"Volunteer?" I echoed.

"Yes, she read practice interview questions to our clients. We serve women who have difficult home lives. Often, they are victims of domestic violence. Women who are often now homeless, living in shelters. Many times, they have never worked, having been stay-at-home moms. Candace helped these women practice their interview skills. We also help them create resumes before applying for jobs. But Candace's involvement was relatively new. She'd only been assisting for a couple of months."

Roddy nodded. "And you know all the volunteers?"

Ms. Jenkins smiled as she shook her head no. "Oh no, we have lots of people who help. They come and go. But I remember Candace because she donated money last month. Wrote us a check for $1,000. I stopped by and personally thanked her. She seemed embarrassed by the additional attention."

I looked at Roddy. "Makes sense. Right after she came into her money."

"How many people work here?" I asked.

Ms. Jenkins said, "Full-time? Just four of us. But we have forty volunteers at any one time. Businesswomen, doctors, psychiatrists, social workers, and lots of church women. Some men help too, of course." She smiled to let us know she was being charitable with her words, but her look told us not many men passed through these doors—and fewer still were trusted.

"Do you have any idea where Candace Grabber and her daughter might have gone? Or know of anyone here who might have assisted her?"

Ms. Jenkins kept up her perky mood but offered no assistance. "No," she said, "I only spoke to her personally that one time. I'm sorry I can't help."

We returned to the truck afterwards and saw the data bank growing from the Stingray collecting cell phone calls from the building in front of us. We waited an hour, watching the data flow in, then headed back to the office. But analyzing the data would have to wait. When we returned to Third and Figueroa, Calvin Grabber stood outside our locked office door.

I opened the exterior door and we three entered our lobby.

"I want a status report," he said, following as we entered.

My partner gave me a bob of the head, raising the messenger bag containing the Stingray like "you handle this shit" and skedaddled on into my office. He closed the door. I heard the lock click behind him.

Grabber moved in close to my face. Too close. I could feel his hot breath on my face. "Where's he going? What's in that bag?"

My first reaction was to push the man back, but I kept it

under control and moved around Roddy's desk, creating space between us. "It's only been one day. We've been interviewing your wife's known associates. Roddy's examined her emails, her bank statements, your phone records. We may have something, but it's too early in the investigation..."

I shrugged and sat in the lobby chair.

Calvin Grabber cut me off. "What have you got? Who helped her get away?" His face was red. He put those thick wrists of his down on the credenza and leaned toward me. His eyes glowed.

I leaned right back into him. My face nearly touched his. "We got nothin'. Not yet."

"I gave you ten thousand dollars. I demand to know what you have so far." He did not intimidate easily, but nor did I. Roddy would laugh at the scene if he came back into the room.

I took a breath, giving in, but with my point made. "That's not the terms we agreed to. We're not hunting them down for you to drag home. We don't know where they are or even who helped them—if someone did. We might have a lead. That's what Roddy's working on right now. We're good at this. Keep the faith."

Grabber stood up, his point made—he controlled us and he was boss. "Will you call me this evening to let me know if your lead panned out?"

"Sure," I said and motioned toward the door.

Grabber nodded solemnly and exited without another word.

∾

I entered my office after a knock and an unlocking twist to the knob on Roddy's side. "Got anything?"

"Maybe. The perky Sandy Jenkins made two calls in the first five minutes after we left. I'm checking them right now. But it appears the first was to a cosmetic surgeon on Rodeo Drive."

"That's interesting," I said, moving to the desk, adjusting my prosthesis by propping it on the surface as I sat down.

Roddy peered up from his laptop as he used the police reverse phone number directory software he'd stolen. "Second phone call is even more interesting."

"Really? Pray tell, who?"

"LAPD Domestic Violence Major Assault Unit. Hollenbeck Division. Detective named Marla Young."

"A cop?"

"Yeah, a cop."

The next morning, we went to see the plastic surgeon, a Dr. Anthony Maglioni, but he was in surgery and was not expected to be free for at least four hours. We decided not to wait, and instead drove to the Hollenbeck Division cop shop to see Detective Marla Young. She was out and otherwise occupied, but after finding out I had spent seven years on the force, the desk sergeant made a call on our behalf. We met Det. Young at a watering hole on South Spring called Crane's where cops went for lunch. Cool place. The bar was set up in an old bank vault. During daylight hours it was a quiet joint. At ten in the morning, we were the only three customers there. My first take was it looked like Detective Young might know her way around the vault bar here a bit too well. Her face was rosy and her eyes suspicious as we met her near a tabletop poker machine.

Roddy analyzed the situation well. He pulled up a stool and ordered a cold draw and a Jack chaser. He nodded at her, gave her a wink, and surprisingly she responded back with a nod. He waved his finger around and the bartender brought three of each. I plotted out how to question a detective trained in interrogation, but it turned out Detective Marla Young was an easy nut to crack. She wanted to get drunk, or so it seemed. And more than that, she seemed eager to get her secret off her chest.

"A Brand New Me isn't about helping women interview for a job. That is a front," the detective told us within 15 minutes and two drinks. She'd had at least one before we arrived, I could tell, and whatever she was hiding was eating her up inside. Young almost begged us to listen to her story. "It's all by word of mouth. Women who need to get away from their men. You know the type of man. Controlling assholes. Batterers. Abusers. But for the women we help, these assholes usually have enough money and influence to keep the women from getting on with their lives. Sad gals trying to ditch bad guys."

I noticed the "we" in her description. "And Candace Grabber decided to make use of the organization's services?" I asked.

"Yes."

"How's it work?" Roddy asked. He started to motion for more drinks. I stopped him. I thought Detective Young was too intoxicated already. I was worried that with another drink she wouldn't get the details to us correctly.

"There are women who support the program," she said. "Older rich women, so there is money. We use the money to find women who are in hospitals or hospices. A Brand New Me recruits women who have terminal diseases, like cancer or advanced lupus."

Roddy asked, "How do these dying women help? Do you scam them out of their money?"

Detective Young looked at him with a slanted eye. "No, we scam them out of their names."

And then she spilled the beans. It was like her confession was held back by the slenderest of dams, like the membrane on the brim of an overfull pint of beer before the fluid leaked over the side. The tiniest breech could cause a major spill. We couldn't have stopped her telling us the story if we wanted to.

It went like this: Marla Young met Sandy Jenkins, the head counselor at A Brand New Me years ago when the detective brought an abused woman to the nonprofit for help. The organization at that time aided women in finding new homes, new employment, and self-respect. Prior to Detective Young's involvement, most of the organization's clients were in the city's homeless shelters, but the policewoman began to bring A Brand New Me a new type of client —an affluent one, but despite their income, they were still abused and in need of assistance. Over drinks one night, Young and Jenkins created a hypothetical "underground railroad" for the abused women. When the two sobered up the next day, the idea percolated.

Then in the week after, a client was killed by her husband after he found she'd received a suit of clothes from A Brand New Me. The abused woman's plan had been to get a job and leave her husband. He did not allow her that chance. Suddenly, the percolation became a real plan.

Perky Sandy Jenkins was in sales. She developed scouts who found women in hospice or hospital care who were terminally ill and without family attending to them. The counselor assembled recruiters in the Los Angeles area hospice community to seek these lonely survivors out. It sounded impossible to find these kind of women in numbers, but Det. Young assured me I was wrong. There are 18 million people in the greater Los Angeles area, she said. Of that, perhaps one percent die each year—most of natural causes. Of that 18,000, roughly 8,500 are female. Most are elderly. Of those, 90 percent have family by their side, but still just under one hundred each year, Sandy Jenkins discovered, were terminally ill and on their own. They had outlived their spouses and had no one left who looked after them. It was to these women each year that A Brand New Me's' underground railroad reached out.

The play was sweet. These dying women could give the gift of life to another woman, one who needed a new start, a new identity. The terminally ill women must agree to die anonymously as a ward of the state—which was a short step from the death they were currently facing.

If the woman agreed, she was moved to the city's hospice for the medically indigent. Her intake papers said "Jane Doe." She was listed as suffering from dementia, no identity available, having been found by police on the streets. The police, in each case, was, of course, Detective Marla Young. Each indigent woman was given a medical work-up. The diagnosis was already known to be terminal. Each was placed in the hospice with a wink and a nod. The now indigent woman would die with dignity, knowing her name would live on with another woman, one running from her abusive husband or partner. The ole switch-o-change-o.

That was step one. Step two was the client, who was now on the run and might be considered missing or the victim of foul play, would be hidden in a safe house. Off the radar. Then step three would be put into play. The client would receive cosmetic surgery, altering her facial features and even providing liposuction or breast augmentation. Stylists were brought into the safe house to provide new hair colors, new cuts, and a fresh look after sufficient healing had taken place after the cosmetic surgery. Personal shoppers provided new clothing. No expense was spared; no vestige of the client's past was allowed to remain.

Step four was the use of a forger to provide an updated driver's license with a photo of the client's new face. The social security card of the deceased was still good as her death had gone unreported. Usually, the credit of the previous owner of the identity had been strained by the medical bills of the terminally ill, but there were the other benefactors who pledged money to this women's underground railroad. The few who were recruited while still having some assets gave them to the organization.

When Marla Young finished her tale, Roddy bought her one more beer. Her mouth seemed dry and her lips parched from so much talking.

I nodded at her. "And then where do they go? These women you set up for a new life? You just let them walk out the door?"

Marla shook her head. "Most I take down to LAX and put on a plane. One-way ticket purchased with cash."

"And you never hear from them again?" Roddy asked.

"There is an email address Sandy monitors to see if any of them need help. We generally don't hear from them again."

Roddy mused for a second. "How many we talking about over the last three years?"

"Maybe five the first year as we were learning the ropes," said Detective Young. "We moved slow, made sure we got everything right. The next two years 20. Nine the second, and eleven the third. We're just beginning our fourth year of spiriting these women away."

"Who signs the death certificates on the Jane Does?" I asked.

Detective Young narrowed her eyes. "A woman at the county morgue processes for us. She doesn't ask too many questions if the cause of deaths prove to be natural."

"She doesn't know the scam?"

"Doesn't know but has probably figured it out. Doesn't need it spelled out."

"And how do the women get moved to the indigent care unit?

"Ambulance service. Same folks every time. A Brand New Me has them on retainer. We pay well. It's on the up-and-up. The intake papers are switched at the pick-up. Names disappear and the in-take always says Jane Doe. Sandy Jenkins takes care of the switch."

"After the forger does the paperwork?" I chimed in.

"Nah, intakes are easy. Just typed two-page forms. Sometimes I fill them out. Sometimes Sandy."

"And the cosmetic work? Another man-hater wanting to help her sister?" I asked, killing the last of my beer.

Detective Young laughed. "You're a cynical bastard."

"Seven years on the force, three wearing the shield, vice, and homicide."

She nodded. "That explains the cynicism."

Roddy steered her back. "So, you've helped 25 women go off the grid? Accessory before the fact on 25, including the creation of forged legal documents. Faked another 25 death certificates. Defrauded the state of out of hospice and burial expenses for 25 women. Lied to investigating officers, I'm sure, probably the FBI too, again illegal. Filed false police reports. Grace here is better than me at knowing what charges could get filed. I'm sure he could add on for a while."

"You're saying I would be in jail a long time if the shit comes down."

Roddy nodded.

She nodded back. "Before I ask you if it's gonna rain shit today, let me tell you this. I'd do it again. I've worked this job for 23 years. Been on Domestic Abuse for eight years. Saw too many women killed by their partners. Murder. Murder/suicide. Murder, death by cop. In the last three years, I saved twenty-five lives." She looked at me. "You know for sure you saved 25 lives in your career? I do. For damned sure, I do." She placed her fist on the bar.

I shook my head slowly. "Not twenty-five. Not for sure."

Her eyes turned a deeper brown as she raised her face to the two of us. "Should I expect a shit storm? I always knew there might come a day of retribution for breaking a whole stack of laws. Committing crimes. Except I really think I did good, but the D.A. wouldn't think so. If you turn me in, I'm prepared for it."

Roddy shook his head. "Don't worry yourself, lady. We only promised we would find Candace Grabber. We have no reason to drop a dime on you. We just want to make sure that Candace Grabber is okay. We never promised her schmuck of a husband we would tell him where she was. We just want to talk to her. See if she and her daughter are okay."

I stuck out my hand. "Thanks for your service to the city, Detective Young."

"Thanks." Her voice broke and her eyes filled with tears.

"Four things," I said as we both rose to leave. "One, where did Candace Grabber fly off to with her one-way ticket? Two, what name is she going by? And three, what is the name of the cosmetic surgeon you used for Candace Grabber?"

Detective Young raised her chin a bit. "She was the only one who didn't leave L.A. She wanted to live a new life right under the nose of that son-of-a-bitch husband of hers. She just got in a taxi with her daughter and rode away. I got no clue where she is. And since I didn't book the plane ticket, I never got a name either."

Roddy nodded. "The plastic surgeon's name?"

"Anthony Maglioni on Rodeo Drive."

"We thought as much. Only the best, eh?" I said.

"He charges us next to nothing and then writes off the

entire amount in taxes. Ten of 'em a year, he says, and then he pays squat to Uncle Sam in taxes."

Roddy laughed. "We'll add Accessory to Tax Evasion to the list." He turned and walked through the bar, giving me room to get in a last query.

Detective Young looked at me. "You said four things. You only asked me three questions."

"Yeah," I said, "the last one's advice. Get into AA. You're too good a cop to go down the drain with booze."

She nodded. I took a step, then paused again. "You're not gonna give us Candace's new identity? I think you do know it. We're not going to jam you up. You know that, right?"

Detective Young smiled, waving the bartender over for a celebratory last round of her liquid lunch. "I swear I don't know it. I would have if I had booked her a plane ticket. But she didn't want one. Brand New Me's on a need-to-know basis. Sandy would know."

I smiled. "Yeah, well, she's not telling."

Detective Young shrugged.

After sitting for an hour listening to the detective's tale, I limped on my good leg toward the door, following my partner. Sitting for so long had made my stump ache. I heard Detective Young call my name. "Grace, Detective Grace," She used the title I had not heard for a long while.

"Yeah?" I thought she was going to give me the name.

"Be careful with Grabber. He may look like a banker, but he's a cruel, dangerous man. He did awful things to Candace before she left. But nothing we could prove in court. He's bad. Pure bad."

"Gotcha," I said into the daylight, reentering the street. "I kind of figured that one out."

Roddy was behind the wheel of his hand-controlled GMC truck when I joined him outside. A parking ticket was tucked under the windshield wiper. He opened the window, leaned out, turned on the wiper and as the ticket rose with the blade, he grabbed it, wadded it up, and threw it behind the seat of the truck in one motion.

"Not afraid they'll boot your truck for unpaid tickets?" I asked.

Roddy smiled, lighting a cigarette. "Nope, their software is easy to hack. I just go in and change the ticket over to paid. Easy-peezy."

I shook my head and laughed.

"Where to, Captain, oh Captain?" he asked, joining me.

I pointed west. "Rodeo Drive. Dr. Anthony Maglioni, cosmetic surgeon and tax evader."

"Thought you'd say that."

Dr. Maglioni's office was a single door leading off the street in the 200 block of North Rodeo Drive, not far from Agent Provocateur, a very upscale lingerie place. Roddy smiled as we passed it by, looking for a parking place. "You ever been in there?"

"No, why?"

"Karen got me something for my birthday from there."

"For you?"

"Well, she wore it, but yeah, it was for me."

"Getting close to TMI, Rod. But I'm happy for you. Karen is a keeper. Hey, look there, a handicapped parking spot."

Roddy expertly navigated into the space, pulled the permit from the side pocket in the door, and hung it from the mirror. We ambled down the block, watching ever-so-thin women with augmented breasts leave the doctor's office and head into the lingerie store. We both smiled.

Maglioni made us wait for a bit, but then a male receptionist, tall, thin and snotty, led us to a mahogany-paneled office. Maglioni was everything a cosmetic surgeon on Rodeo Drive should be—mannered, Italian accented, prosperous with a tiny speck of greed hanging from his sleeve. "Gentlemen, gentlemen, Silas gave me your cards. The Purple Heart Detective Agency. Who has not heard of you from the papers? What can I do for you?"

The doctor gently shook our hands and directed us to sit in bright red chairs, the leather arms so soft the breasts he worked on would have seemed like sandpaper in comparison.

"We just had a lengthy conversation with Detective Marla Young. She told us quite a story."

Roddy was silent, letting me do the talking.

"I see. And you have questions for me?" The smile was gone off Maglioni's face, but his composure was in place.

"Yes. We understand you are part of an 'underground railroad' type organization which is helping abused women set up new lives for themselves. You help them change their looks to evade their abusive spouses."

"I do nothing of the kind."

"Well, according to Detective Young," I started, but he cut me off.

"I do charitable work for A Brand New Me, an organization which helps abused women. They come to me with medical certificates from a licensed physician on staff there. I provide my services at cost, which are paid by donations to the non-profit. All my actions are strictly above board."

"Except none of the women are using their real names."

"So, you say." Maglioni smiled, taking some hand lotion from his desk and applying a tiny drop to each palm. He motioned to each of us if we should like some. We declined. "I assure you this conversation is the first time I have heard of such affairs. It sounds so like a conspiracy theory to me. Like a delicious movie plot, don't you think?"

"Not really. And we really don't care about your arrangement with the organization or any tax benefits you might get from working with them."

The good doctor blanched at my jibe, but then shrugged it off. He did not respond.

"We're just looking for one woman. Mrs. Candace Grabber," Roddy said and leaned across the table and handed the good doctor her photo.

"Have you treated her?" Roddy asked.

"Classic overbite, weak chin. Poorly defined cheekbones. Easy fixes really."

"Yes, I'm sure," Roddy replied, "but did you work on her?"

"I'm sure," Maglioni said, his smile both effacing and

deferential in tandem, "you are aware privacy laws forbid me from telling you anything about a patient's medical records —if Ms. Grabber was a patient, which I cannot confirm or deny."

"So, you're not giving us shit," Rod said with just a hint of hostility.

Maglioni smiled greasily. "Oh no," he laughed. "I think that's exactly what I'm giving you."

Afterwards, Roddy and I went to our favorite bar, Sundowners, a darkly paneled afterhours place with the longest running poker game in L.A. going on in the back. Our buddy Rat was already at the table, having arrived before we did. He waved, but his cards must have been good, because his sunglasses went right back down after he greeted us. He was into the game and it was how he earned his living so he'd better be into it.

We got a table off to ourselves. Roddy ordered a Widow Jane with a splash. "What the hell is that?" I asked.

"Good new bourbon. Made in Brooklyn."

"Because all the good bourbon is made in... Brooklyn. I'll take mine from Kentucky. Give me a Wellers," I said to the server who knew us but left us be after taking our orders.

Roddy smiled. I knew that smile. My partner had an idea. "What's in that brain pan of yours, compadre?" I asked.

Roddy didn't speak. He just sat there listening to the bar stereo play "In a Sentimental Mood" by Duke Ellington with John Coltrane on the sax. Roddy stayed just like that with a shit-eating grin on his face until our drinks arrived. He ordered a second round as she set down our first. Roddy took a tiny sip, approved, and then took a big swig.

"Spill it."

"No way. Do you have any idea how much this stuff costs?"

"Your idea, smart ass. Spill it."

Roddy smiled and spoke, his voice honey after the smooth whisky. "A Brand New Me is a non-profit. A 501(c)(3). That means their donors are public record. We can check the names of the women who have donated to the organization. That list is likely to have the names of the dying women who were recruited to give up their identities. We can cross reference the names on the list to known addresses. Those who have obvious public records we eliminate. Those who do not, we track down their photo from the California DMV. We'll use my bootleg FBI facial recognition software to try to establish a match between the photos on the driver's licenses of the women who now have those names and Candace Grabber's photo. See if we get a match."

"Any idea how many women might donate to A Brand New Me?"

"Not a clue, but I bet it's a lot. But the computer will do the work eliminating the wrong faces. We just run down the photos on those we can't find a virtual record for. Most people will post their shit on-line. Facebook, Twitter, you know, 21st century stuff." Roddy paused, "Oh no, I guess you wouldn't." He laughed. I am not very into tech and social media. He rarely lets me forget it.

Our second round of drinks arrived and we took our

time. Rat came over with his winnings and bought a third round. Then Roddy waved us off. "Now I'm too drunk to drive us home. I'm a father now, you know. Can't go around driving drunk."

Rat smiled. "That was my first. I'll take you."

Since Karen was gone with little Gracie and Jerry the monkey to visit her parents in Scottsdale, I also crashed at Roddy's place for the night. Dapper the coyote could do without me for a night. An hour and a pizza later, Karen called with her nose a little out of joint after Roddy answered the phone drunk (we had a couple more once we arrived at the house), but she complemented Rod on catching a ride home while intoxicated and decided it was a step toward maturity. A truce was declared and the conversation, at least the portion I heard, became less accusatory. "Baby steps, baby," he was telling her as he carried the phone up the stairs, cooing at her. Then I slid off to my home away from home, the spare bedroom, and slept.

When I woke up, it looked as if Roddy had been working on his computer all night. He sat in boxer shorts at the kitchen island, pounding away at the keyboard. A vial of Adderall was open with pills spilled on the counter. He did not look up as I entered. "I'll have something for us in about two hours. You'll need to go after one of our vehicles. Mine is at the bar. Yours is at the office. There's a twenty by the coffee maker. Get a dozen donuts at Blinkie's Donut Emporium on Topanga Canyon Blvd before you come back."

I saluted him. "Aye-aye, Captain."

Roddy looked up, laughing.

"You sure you weren't an officer back in over in the sand-box?" I asked. "You sure sound like a brass ass."

"Sorry, I'm on a roll." He nodded at the pills. "I down-loaded Brand New Me's annual reports and all the monthly addendums. I found a list of women donors. I'm cross-refer-encing them against new driver's licenses issued in Califor-nia's DOT. Also, I'm checking any social media for photos of the women before and after the issuance of driver's licenses. Also checking medical records. Then eliminating any women whose records were issued before Candace went missing. Later I'll use her photo as the template for a facial recognition program with all the women in the database of the non-profit. I will cross-reference that program with all the photos again. Then we'll see if we can narrow the list down. Right now, I've got about three hundred donors. I have no idea if it will work or if we'll get anyone who looks even a little bit like Candace Grabber that fits our time window."

I nodded, getting it. "And if we figure out a name, we'll have a leg up on finding her. If—and that is a big 'if'—she is still in Southern California. It could be she didn't trust Detective Marla Young to keep her mouth shut about her destination."

"Which would have shown pretty good instincts as it turns out," Rod replied.

"Yep," I agreed. "It would have. Maybe Candace, with her new name, took a bus to San Diego and bought a one-way ticket for the two of them to Toledo, Ohio."

"And if she did that, we got no shot. Not if they're living off the grid. Living on cash."

"And she's got a suitcase full of freaking cash."

Roddy's eyes went back to the laptop screen. "So, get us some wheels and don't come back without the donuts.

"Sir, yes, sir." I grabbed the twenty off the bar and headed out the door, dialing Uber as I went. The morning was nice and I would sit outside for my ride.

Forty minutes later, Uber dropped me at the office. I went up to check mail and messages before getting the jeep and heading back to Roddy's. The phone on the desk rang as I entered.

"Get those bloodstains off your cuffs?" said the voice, a male's.

"Who is this?"

"I'm sorry. It's Father Bregoli. I'm afraid I made a bad joke —you know the tomato juice. Your comeback stung me the other day. I guess I brushed you off a bit harshly. And now that appears to have been a bad mistake."

"Oh, hello," I replied. "A bad mistake? Why?"

"Well, Calvin Grabber just called. He made a scene at A Brand New Me, raising... well, raising a ruckus, and now he's headed our way. He sounded quite angry. Violently so. I was thinking of calling the police, but I still had your card and thought of calling you first."

"Okay, if he's raising hell before I get there, do call the cops. Don't take a chance. I'm in my office right now, but I'll hurry. I'm a bit closer to you than Grabber is right now if he just left Brand New Me. I'm on my way."

It took only 20 minutes to get to the rectory since I ran some lights and raced way over the speed limit, but Grabber beat me there. I could hear him bellow from the foyer of the rectory office as I entered.

"You. You're her best friend," he shouted. "It was either you who helped her or you know who did. I know you did. I'm sure of it." Grabber's voice was thick with malevolence. I stepped inside the door of the office. The beefy man was doing his lean-over-the-desk intimidation trick. He towered over the receptionist like a red-eyed vulture. His voice was tremulous and full of menace. "Tell me, damn it," he said.

I interceded, pulling his shoulder that he should face me. His first reaction was to swing, but he resisted. I motioned with my hand for him to join me in the hallway. I decided to play a bluff, to give Grabber a red herring to grab onto, remembering something in the reports Roddy put together after examining the family's computer. "Mr. Grabber, a word please."

He looked at me, confused that I should be there. "Not now. They know something and they're not telling. They must..."

I interrupted him. "Roddy and I have a real lead. We found someone who's seen them," I lied.

His eyes raised. He had taken the bait. His head turned, though his frame stayed over the desk, leaning into the frightened woman's face. "What?"

"Let's step outside. Privacy?" I said, turning my back, leaving the antechamber.

He joined me red-faced on the front step. "'What have you learned?"

"Did you take a woman to Palm Desert? Last winter, did you take a woman, not your wife, to Palm Desert?"

Grabber looked dumbfounded. "No, of course not. I did go there. I went there for a conference last winter, but I was alone."

"But you stayed offsite? Casa Larrea Inn or something like that? Ordered wine to your room? Like you were socializing."

"Yes, that hotel was much cheaper than the conference resort rate. I met another member of the board there. He wanted wine. I did not object. And what has wine to do with my wife's disappearance?"

"Candace was seen in several women's apparel stores in the Beverly Center Mall," I lied. "She was buying resort wear, swimsuits, tennis garb, things like that. We canvassed with Candace's and your daughter's photos. The clerks remembered her. Large purchases for cash, headed to Palm Desert. She mentioned to one of the nuns that she saw your hotel bill. Candace said she was going to see if she could find the bimbo you were with, to use her words. Said 'two can play at that game.'" I laid it on thick. "Did she get it wrong? Did you not have a woman with you up there?"

Grabber was stunned. "Of course not. I told you. It was a financial conference. Our annual state meeting. We always have it at a resort out of season. I was with Dennis Malone. Candace knows him quite well. Oh my God. Do you think she's up there right now?"

"We have a man canvassing the various resorts with their

photos," I fibbed. "There are dozens of hotels out there and if she's paying cash, there'll be no record. The best places are very discreet, so people aren't going to talk."

"Did you try Casa Larrea?"

"Yeah, she's not there."

Grabber looked perplexed. I realized then he may have been up late drinking. His face looked bloated, flesh puckered around those eyes of his, puffy, dark, but still formidable. I thought he was hungover. "What are you going to do?" he asked.

"Maybe it would help if you went there and looked for her yourself," I said, baiting the hook.

"To Palm Desert? Today?"

"People will be more forthcoming to a husband and father than a couple of private snoops," I offered.

He nodded. "I'll have to rearrange my schedule. Are you coming down too?"

"No, now that we have a promising idea where she is, Roddy is doing some computer work on a variety of the resorts, phone records and so forth. Maybe Candace will leave a computer record for us to find. I'm recanvassing the people we've interviewed to see if they can narrow down where your wife and daughter are hiding out. That's why I'm here." I looked over my shoulder at the receptionist behind him. "And you didn't make that any easier. It looks like you scared the shit out of that woman. Don't make my job harder, Calvin," I said, using his Christian name for the first time, trying to draw him closer to me, to foster false allegiance. "Stay away from people who might be harboring her or harboring information about her."

"You really think I should go to Palm Desert and show Candace and Sherry's photos around? It seems like something you should be doing."

I shook my head. "People will be much more receptive to you. And it won't do any good for you to talk to her friends. She's poisoned them against you. They won't tell you anything. I'll manage them. Have you been anywhere else?"

He looked sheepishly at me. "I just came from A Brand New Me."

"Who'd you yell at?"

He smiled at that. "That bossy one. Skinny counselor."

"Sandy Jenkins?"

"Yeah, her. She knew something too. Her face was all sad for a moment. Then angry. I know she wasn't telling me something."

"Let me handle her. How soon can you get to Palm Desert? We do need your help up there. Roddy will call you if he gets anything off the computer searches."

Grabber met my eyes. "I'll have to go to the office, get my secretary to reschedule my appointments for the next few days. Then I'll go home and pack. I can be there by late evening." He turned and left without another word. He was a man not big on goodbyes.

With Grabber out of the way, I left without talking to the priest or anyone else at the rectory. Then I picked up the donuts and went back to Roddy's to feed the bear some bear claws.

"I've got six possibilities. Tonya Tannin, Elizabeth Vanner, Kim Barnes—plus three Jane Does."

I brushed powdered sugar off my nose. "Okay, and what have you learned about those six?"

"Weird stuff. And that's what's strange. Tannin and Barnes were both issued new driver's licenses, but not Vanner. Tannin, Vanner, and Barnes all had cosmetic work done by good Dr. Maglioni. She's listed as a new donor for Brand New Me. She's listed as getting a nose job, but there's no new California I.D. There were six death certificates issued at the morgue last month on Jane Does—all delivered from the city's indigent hospice. I would think three of those were the real Tannin, Vanner, and Barnes. I know nothing about the three extra stiffs."

"And as regards to the facial recognition program?" I asked.

"Vanner and Barnes are both wearing glasses in their driver's license photos on the DMV website, so the best the computer could do was give me a partial. Neither woman was ruled out, but the Vanner photo on her license is an old one, issued before Candace Grabber disappeared."

"So that would appear to rule Vanner out unless a new driver's license shows up. How about Tannin?" I inquired.

"She's black, so I'm guessing she's out."

I laughed. "Yeah, I guess Maglioni is not that good at cosmetic surgery."

Roddy motioned at the box of donuts and I handed him another. He scarfed it up in three bites. "Any electronic records on Barnes or the Jane Does? Something to give us a place to start?" I asked.

Roddy shrugged. "Nothing except the two mugshots in the DMV system." He showed me the first photo. A 40-year-old woman with geometric spiky red hair. She wore tortoise-shelled brown glasses. Her face was fair. She did not have buck teeth. She was not attractive. Her jawline was not weak. Not someone you would give a second glance to on the street.

Could it be Candace Grabber? I realized she'd had cosmetic surgery, someone had dyed and cut her hair, bought her new clothes, and taught her how to apply her makeup. I looked at the photo of Candace Grabber on the desk and then at the DMV shot of Kim Barnes on the computer. I didn't think it was her. Maybe I was wrong.

Roddy switched the screen to the second photo. This photo showed a large woman, blonde, messy hair, with some gray working its way into the mix.

"Who's this?"

Roddy glanced over at the screen. "That's Elizabeth Vanner's photo. Taken three years ago. She gave about two hundred grand to A Brand New Me two months ago. Like I said, we have records that she got cosmetic work done and it was billed to A Brand New Me, but I'm guessing it was someone else using her ID. I'm guessing the woman in this photo is dead."

"But no new driver's license issued with a new photo?"

"No, not here or anywhere in the states. Candace could have taken the name but then decided not to get a new license. Could have run to Mexico with a suitcase full of cash, I suppose."

"Then we won't find her."

He agreed.

"And you got nothing on the Jane Does—nothing except we got three more bodies than we got names."

"Yep, thought my searching might clear things up, but it gave us more questions than answers. What's next?" Roddy asked with his mouth full of donut. He washed it down with cold coffee. The pot had long since turned itself off.

"Well, Detective Young seems to know how each woman started her journey. Let's suppose she was right. Candace wanted to stay local. Maybe we can eliminate some of the names by seeing where they went. Let's check the names against plane tickets. Search for Elizabeth Vanner and Kim Barnes for plane flights. Let's see if we can find a plane ticket booked in the last 60 days for either name. We might be able to eliminate one of them that way."

Roddy long ago created backdoors to the airlines' booking lists so it was a quick search. We found Kim Barnes booked a flight to Miami, Florida, connecting on a commuter to Marathon, Florida. It looked like Kim might be planning to start anew in Key West or somewhere near there. For now, we agreed Barnes was out. And besides, I didn't think the photo was that of Candace Grabber with a new face.

Detective Young said Candace refused to leave town. However, the fact there was no new driver's license was concerning, but we only had the one name left on the list. Elizabeth Vanner was now the target of our search.

"So where do we find Elizabeth Vanner?" Roddy asked, still munching on donuts. He moved to the fridge, opening a bottle of California brewed specialty beer called Lost Abbey. Finishing the pastry in his hand, Roddy then lifted the last remaining with the other and took a bite. Then more beer. "Good stuff, Maynard."

I laughed, took the bottle from his hand, and took a swig. "Damn, that's good," I said. "Got another?" What the hell! It was noon—in Denver.

He nodded to the fridge. "So where next?"

I shrugged, opening my own Lost Abbey. "How 'bout we go back to Ms. Sandy Jenkins? Test Elizabeth Vanner's name on her. See if we get a reaction."

"Okay, and if that doesn't work, we tackle Detective Young for a second go." He paused. "You know it's a little weird how tore up Marla Young is over all of this when everyone else has been so hard core."

"You think she's in deeper emotionally than the others in some way?"

Roddy shrugged. "I don't know. Some people can't hold their sin—just like some people can't hold their booze."

"And you think Marla Young is a teetotaler regarding the consumption of sin? Seems unlikely for someone who's made detective. She would have certainly seen a ton of it on the way up on L.A.'s mean streets. She should be able to hold it together by now—no matter how awful the headlines in her head might get."

"Can't say for sure. Know we're both good at it."

I laughed and took another drink. "That is not a compliment."

"Didn't say it was."

∿

Sandy Jenkins was in a pink suit when we dropped in on her day. We could see her standing outside her office, watching us walk toward her. It was past lunch, but she was still drinking coffee. She held a cream-colored Starbucks ceramic travel mug with the button lid. Steam curled from its top whenever she raised it to her pink lip-sticked smackers.

"We're back," Roddy announced as we bypassed the receptionist and walked straight back to Ms. Jenkins' office.

"How wonderful for us all," Jenkins said factiously.

"In detective parlance, this is called a 'follow-up,'" said Roddy, taking the lead this time. "We have a couple more questions. Perhaps you could help us."

She smiled ruefully. "I already told you I don't have any information on Candace Grabber for you. I have no idea where she is. And after that awful man, Calvin Grabber, was in here yesterday yelling and making threats there is no way I'd help you two lead him to Candace. That will never happen."

"Yeah," I responded," sorry about that. Our understanding with him is we'll find Candace and the daughter Sherri, make sure they're okay, but we won't tell him where they are. Mr. Grabber is a bit intense."

"He's abusive."

"Probably," I said. "But he deserves to know if his daughter is okay. We said we would do that much. What can you tell us about Elizabeth Vanner? Do you know where she is?"

My jarring segue got a reaction. Ms. Jenkins' body jerked a bit and her eyes popped. It was what social scientists call a revelatory micro-expression—almost a macro. The woman regained her composure in a nanosecond, but she knew we knew she'd given herself away. Bingo.

She countered to cover her faux-paux. "Not after the way Grabber behaved in here yesterday. You get nothing from me."

"The husband's not in town. I sent him on a wild goose chase. He's checking hotel registries in Palm Desert for his wife and child. Evidently," I winked, "there was a Candace Grabber sighting up there in the last couple of days."

"I highly doubt that," Sandy Jenkins replied with a tart reply.

Roddy and I both stared at her. Her face bloomed red and she rolled her eyes toward the ceiling. Jenkins sighed with great lament and motioned us into her office. We entered and she closed the door.

"So, by your comment," Roddy asked, soft-pedaling, "you do know where she is?"

Sandy Jenkins said with a whisper, "I can't give up her name or where she is. I vowed I would never, ever, do that— even upon penalty of imprisonment. I am certainly not telling you two. I 'm sorry. You seem like decent guys, but Candace Grabbers' husband is a beast. I won't tell."

"You know we could blow the whole organization up. Give it to the cops. Give it to the *L.A. Times*."

She nodded. "I said I thought you were decent guys. You do that, tell the authorities, then good people, including me and Marla, go to jail. And the women we helped will be dragged back to their abusive partners. You will be the force that results in them being killed."

"We know that and we agree you are on the side of the

angels," Roddy said. "But we have to know the two of them are okay. We need to talk to both Candace and Sherri. You don't know us very well, but we don't fucking quit. We'll keep at it. You'll eventually tell us, screw up, or we'll be in your lobby area to question you every morning. You think you'll be able to help women with two detectives setting up shop in your reception area?"

Jenkins sighed again. "Okay, maybe we can meet partway. Are you two willing to go someplace with me? You'd have to wear blindfolds until we got there. Ride in the back of a panel van where you can't see out. You up for that?"

Roddy met my glance. "Sure," we both said at the same time. "Let's do it."

Sandy Jenkins laughed. "You aren't even going to ask where I'm taking you?"

Roddy laughed. "Lady, I figure you ain't going to shoot us in the head and leave our bodies in Sepulveda Basin after dark."

Jenkins laughed. "You think not? You are too trusting." Then she led us out back to a white paneled van.

Roddy and I got in the back and waited until a woman we'd never seen before moved behind the wheel. Sandy Jenkins closed the curtain to the front of the vehicle as the three of us sat on the floorboards of the bare van. She handed a blindfold to me and indicated I should place it on Roddy's face. I did and then Jenkins applied a second blind-fold to me. The blindfolds were strips cut from black t-shirts doubled for thickness. Once on, they completely obliterated our vision.

At first, I tried to figure out our destination as we moved

from Burbank south, but I lost track of the turns. I know after a while I could hear approaching airport traffic overhead and I knew we were someplace close to LAX, maybe El Segundo or the like. The journey took about 45 minutes of midday traffic, but eventually we slowed turning up a drive with a steep incline. I heard a garage door rise. We went in. The van came to a stop. I heard a garage door go down and we were at our destination.

Sandy Jenkins said, "We're at our safe house. Please don't attempt to leave the inside of the house or look outside the windows. We have blackout curtains throughout. There are currently three women here awaiting the beginning of their new lives. They will be afraid of you. They are afraid of men. Please do not speak to them. If you have questions, ask me and I'll address them. Are you both okay with these terms?"

"Is Candace Grabber here?"

"No," answered Sandy Jenkins. "She spent several weeks here, but she has been gone for at least a month now. None of the women here ever met her."

We nodded. Our eyes were still adjusting to the dim light of the garage. We exited the van and followed Sandy Jenkins into the house. It was a large split level. It was furnished, but the furniture was awful—obviously rescued from the dump or off the curb. Everything inside the home was mismatched castoffs. This residence was not equipped for comfort. It was a passing through station. The women who stayed were not encouraged to stay. This safe house was a train station on an underground railroad.

Sandy yelled up the second level. Eventually, she gathered the three women to the living room and we stood before them. They cowered with trepidation before us—the first men they'd encountered since they disappeared. All were around 40 years of age. One wore two black eyes. Another had her nose packed with cotton. The third wore horn-rimmed glasses and did not meet our gaze.

Roddy tilted his head to me. His fingers raised three fingers for only me to see.

"Have all three of these women here been abused?" I asked Sandy.

Jenkins answered affirmatively, but her role of intermediary was unnecessary. The women answered for themselves, anxious to tell us what horrid men they were with until the last few weeks. They took turns telling their stories. Roddy and I did not speak and simply let them get their words on record. Testifying against their abusive partners.

"Why are your eyes blackened?" Roddy asked. "Did your man hit you?"

"No," said the blonde, "I had work done. Changin' things up before I start over. New hair color too. They say blondes have more fun. I figure to. I haven't had much fun up to now." Her voice revealed a southern drawl that California living had not been able to strip away.

The third woman in the glasses asked us, "Why are you here? Are you police?"

"No," I said, "we're just looking for one of the women who used to stay here?"

Sandy Jenkins smiled patiently. "Do you ladies think anyone who has come through this safe house wants to be found? Do any of you want to tell these men your old names? Where you came from?"

They laughed at us for the ridiculous thought that any of them would want to return to the hell which had been their lives before A Brand New Me rescued them.

Soon our interview was over. The women left the room, returning to their bedrooms and out of our sight. "So?" said Sandy Jenkins, "do you see why I can't give you any information on any of these women? I can't and won't divulge any information. I won't let these women down."

"Regardless if we blow your organization up?"

Sandy Jenkins stared at Roddy without speaking after he asked the question. "I saw your face just now. I am banking on the humanity in you not to do that. I believe I'm a good judge of character. You two aren't going to turn us in." She knew from our silence she was right.

Then she took us back, blindfolded in a van, to our vehicle. And that was that.

On the way back to Roddy's place, I glanced over at him as we traveled from Burbank to Malibu. "What can we do when we can't leverage the behavior of A Brand New Me's people because they know our threats are empty ones? That we won't go to the cops? I'm guessing you agree that we aren't going to turn them in?"

"Hell no," Roddy answered. "I feel like we ought to write 'em a check, not turn 'em in."

"Agreed. So, what's next?" I asked my partner.

"Let me do my computer work once everyone goes to bed

tonight. Karen and Gracie will be home by the time we get there. Maybe I can find something."

I drove home to the trailer in Topanga for the night. I prepared good steaks on the grill for both my semi-pet coyote Dapper and me. The coyote drifted down into the clearing by the trailer at dusk after I arrived home and started the grill. I filled his water bowl with a tray of ice cubes and he occasionally took a sip while he waited for his steak. Dapper seemed to know my head was full of conflicted thoughts so he tried to cheer me up. He went down to the concrete pool and rolled onto his back, waiting for me to come and give him a quick scrub with Dawn dishwater soap I kept in a bottle there. Dapper allowed me to scratch his belly, rinse him and put on a new flea collar. Then after shaking water over me, he trotted to the trailer and lay on the cool metal steps. I joined him and sat on the first step, finishing a beer, and watching the sun fall over the hills of Topanga.

When I moved inside for the evening, he followed me in and lay on the cool laminated floor as the air conditioner hummed on high. I put on Ronnie Woods' "Gimmee Some Neck" and cleaned my guns with an oily rag until I was tired enough to sleep. Dapper curled in a ball at the foot of my bed, his nose aimed at the door, ever vigilant, ready to bolt through the dog door's opening I had installed for his use.

I slept fitfully, dreaming of a safe house filled with women with black eyes, packed noses, and fear in their hearts. I did not rest well and was awake when the phone rang at not quite 5:00 am. Dapper jolted to movement with the first ring and was out the dog door into the night. I knew I would not see him again until the sun fell once again. He was gone, back to the pack that gathered in the hills high up above Mulholland. It was good Dapper still ran with his pack when I was away. I was away a lot. I picked up the phone, expecting it to be Roddy. It was.

"What you got?" I asked.

"A body."

"What?"

"A body," Roddy repeated. "Elizabeth Vanner was cremated in Tulsa, Oklahoma, her hometown, three weeks ago."

"What the fuck? But the real Elizabeth Vanner was buried in a potter's field by L.A. County, right?"

"Yeah, well, someone else got burned to a crisp in Tulsa. Probably Candace. Get down here." He hung up.

I hightailed it down to Malibu in record time, beating morning rush hour traffic to the punch for once.

It was already normal business hours in Tulsa, Oklahoma, which was on central time, when I arrived at Roddy's. We were able to talk by phone to the funeral home director who answered on the first ring. He told us he himself worked on Elizabeth Vanner's body when it arrived by air transport to the funeral home from Los Angeles. He told us the deceased was shipped from the Los Angeles city morgue, funds paid by an anonymous donor according to the notes in his Vanner file, which he forwarded to us by email as we spoke.

"I see," I said into the speaker phone over my cup of coffee as Roddy printed the documents in the folder. "Does the manifest for the body give a cause of death?"

"Oh yes," said the mortician in a patronizing tone, "all shipping of a deceased person requires a standard death certificate which includes cause of death."

"And can you go to the record and tell us what it was? I don't see that document."

"Oh, I don't need to do that. I remember quite well. It was a fractured skull caused by blunt force trauma. Car accident. I remember it quite well because of the damage to Ms. Vanner's face. It was quite unusual. Horrible damage, although she must have had some money."

"Why do you say that?"

"Well, as I said she died of blunt force trauma, but she'd had substantial cosmetic work done just before her death. There had been no healing whatsoever. Excellent work too, expensive. But then, in contrast, her nose was a mess, broken and smashed beyond any repair. I was relieved the instructions were for cremation. We would not have been able to have an open casket service. I guess it didn't matter too much since she only had a single person at the service. Not one family member. And I don't think the one mourner even signed the register. Sad thing, isn't it? To die so alone without a single friend or family member in attendance."

"Was the person who attended the service a little girl about ten?"

"Oh no," replied the mortician. "It was a police officer. A

lady cop from L.A who accompanied Ms. Vanner's remains upon their final journey. She seemed to care very much about Ms. Vanner. Cried quite a lot. I must say I was impressed. You know, Los Angeles police have had such bad press in the last few years."

"Spill it," Roddy growled at the female detective coming off duty. She'd almost made it to her car after her shift. We stood by her vehicle, flanking the female detective.

Detective Marla Young looked at Roddy with surprise. It was not yet eight a.m. and I could see fatigue in the detective coming off third shift. I knew that fatigue. At first, her eyes just registered the amazement that we were there, but then the fatigue of the night shift rapidly to defeat. Then they moved to sadness and resignation. Marla Young nodded, stopping just feet before she reached us. She said, "Not here." She glanced around to see if anyone noticed us, but we were alone. "Somewhere I can get a drink."

We found a 24-hour Irish joint far enough from the station that no cops frequented it. No one frequented it at 8:15 in the morning. Detective Young slid into a booth. The bartender knew her from other mornings after other night shifts. She ordered a Jim Beam double.

"What do you know?" she asked in a deadpan voice as her bourbon and our two coffees arrived.

"That you attended Elizabeth Vanner's funeral in Tulsa, Oklahoma three weeks ago. Except it wasn't Elizabeth Vanner because Elizabeth Vanner died at the city's indigent hospice about a month before that. It was Candace Grabber cremated in Tulsa. She died of blunt force trauma. Beaten to death, but the death certificate falsely reported it as a car wreck. That's what we think. We'll be able to prove it eventually if we must. So, is it true?" Roddy's eyes sparked fire as he accused her.

Detective Marla Young began to cry. She wept aloud and the bartender started to walk over, but Roddy waved a hand menacingly his way and the barkeep veered away from the table in response.

"Partly, yes." She paused. Her voice caught as she spoke. Then she bawled audibly. We were the only customers in the joint and there was no pity at our table. The barkeep kept his eyes off of us. Roddy can be scary.

"And it was her husband? He found her at the safe house and killed her and you let him get away with it. To save your underground railroad operation—to save all your asses, you let him get away with murder."

Detective Young sat forward. Her face registered complete shock and confusion. "No," she said in a whisper. "You got it all wrong. She died on the operating table at Maglioni's on Rodeo Drive. The volunteer doctor over at A Brand New Me gave her a cursory physical, signed her health certificate, and cleared her for cosmetic surgery prior to her appointment. The day she died, Maglioni started his surgery on her eyes, getting rid of her sagging eyelids. Next, he was going to give her a nose job and fix that overbite of hers, but the clinic doctor missed a hairline fracture at her temple. I figure it was from the last beating that son-of-a-bitch of a husband gave her. When Maglioni used the mallet to break her nose, the impact caused the fracture to split on her skull and she died within a minute. Nothing he could do."

It took a minute or so for that to sink in. I was silent, but my partner was not. Roddy snorted in disgust. "Let me guess the next part. You waited until dark and then smuggled the body out like so much medical waste. You took her to the morgue where you already had a co-conspirator lined up and made out a fake death certificate. Then you shipped the body off to her 'quote/unquote' hometown where you knew nobody was left to give a good goddamn."

"Yes," she gasped and waved to the bar man for another drink. This time Roddy let him approach the table.

The bartender set the drink down. "Everything okay over here?"

I glared at him. "So, fucking not okay you cannot imagine. Now beat it."

He retreated.

Roddy stared back at Detective Young until she couldn't hold his gaze. She dropped her eyes to the double in front of her. She took a slug and kept her eyes on the floor.

"You let two doctors walk on malpractice resulting in death charges to cover your sorry drunken ass?"

Detective Young just nodded. Thirty seconds passed. Then she said, "Maglioni demanded we indemnify him against any legal action that might be forthcoming or he was going to go to the cops."

"How did you manage that?" I asked.

"We got him paperwork on LAPD stationary that said Elizabeth Vanner was a protected witness in the WITSEC program and he could not go to the police as it would tip off those against whom she was testifying. He could not report she was dead because it would jeopardize the FBI's attempt to push a plea deal. He would be responsible for putting killers back on the street. Maglioni knew it was bullshit, but he took the letter and filed it with his attorney for protection should he need it."

"Guy's no dummy. He's kept himself pretty insulated all the way through this shit storm," I said.

Detective Young nodded.

"One last question about Candace Grabber," Roddy stated, "before we move on to talk about the daughter."

"Okay," Detective Young was not trying to hide anything now. "What?"

"Maglioni's mallet didn't mess up Elizabeth Vannick's nose so badly that they would have had to have a closed casket service. What the hell happened?"

Detective Young looked at us with tears in her eyes, but it was a fresh look—one of shame. She didn't want to reveal this last horror. Roddy let her stay silent for a second, but then he gripped her arm and began to squeeze, just a little. "Let it all out. You're gonna have to tell it all now—or..." He didn't finish.

"I tried to hide the cosmetic work before we took the body to the morgue. I thought there might be questions..." Her tone was pleading, wanting us to understand.

"You tried to hide it how?" Roddy voice was guttural and fierce.

The air was rarified at our table. Detective Young looked as grim and devastated as anyone I've ever seen. She stared at Roddy as she answered his question. "I hit her face with a phone book. It took a few times." And then Detective Young began to cry, her muffled words descending to a depth like a ship sinking into a very dark and desolate sea.

It took a while for Marla Young to regain a semblance of composure, but we eventually got an address for where Sherri Grabber was being sheltered by the nuns at a convent in Munro Bay, a small village on the ocean just north of San Luis Obispo. We headed there immediately. Looking back as we left the bar, I did not think Detective Young would attempt to thwart us. I did worry she would commit suicide, so as we sped northward, I called Speedy Khuzaymah, a close friend and a detective for the force. I told him Detective Marla Young was in the middle of a mental crisis combined with alcoholic depression and I feared she might harm herself. I gave him the address. He promised to handle it personally. I knew he would—with discretion and sensitivity.

We reached the convent by noon and it was a wonder we didn't get a speeding ticket on the way up. Roddy hauled ass all the way up the PCH.

When we arrived at the convent, a large granite block building with a Spanish style, red ceramic tiled roof, I stood, stretching my leg. My stump ached. The convent was really a castle, or at least a tower and ramparts of white-washed adobe, thick and old. We climbed the steps to the front door, knocked and asked to speak to whomever was in charge. The Mother Superior, we were told politely by the shy, freckly nun who answered the door, would see us in the convent's library. The novice led us to a large room filled with old religious texts. There set a desk and two chairs opposite it in the shadows of the bookshelves.

A nun of about 70 years of age entered. She was stooped with arthritis and had to turn her head to her side to greet us out beyond the white bandeau scarf which held her gray-streaked coif to her head. The woman waved us to sit and we did. She moved slowly, eventually rounded the desk, and sank into a chair. She softly moaned in sitting, such was her pain. The old woman leaned far back so she might meet our eyes without having to arch her bent neck.

"Welcome to our home. I am Sister Alyssa. And you are?"

We told her. Then she asked what she could do for us. We told her that too.

She released to us a muted smile without any humor in it, but still with a dollop of goodwill. "Yes, I always knew someday someone from the rough-and-tumble world we live in would show up and ask about Sherri."

Roddy leaned forward. "Sherri Grabber is here?"

"She is called Sherri Vanner now, but yes, she is here."

"And she is okay?"

Sister Alyssa frowned. "No, I would not say she is okay. She has been through a lot. Her family broke apart. Her father is a violent man who hurt her mother. His violence ultimately led to her death, although indirectly. This young woman has lost all her world. Everything. Well, except her faith. It is a blessing this young lady has unusually strong faith. It has taken all the faith in her heart to get her through this situation even up till now. She is still very fragile."

I nodded solemnly. "She knows her mother is dead?"

"Yes, but not the circumstances, per se. She knows her mother went into the hospital and died. She does not know, nor needs to know, the details. She will be told in time. Years from now. Perhaps it will be me who will tell her. God willing, it will be. If not, the next to oversee the convent will do so."

Roddy looked a bit sheepish. "And the money? Candace Grabber had a half million in cash when she left her husband."

Sister Alyssa frowned. "And is that why you are here? For the money? I am disappointed."

Roddy frowned right back. "No, you misunderstand. Our mission is to make sure the girl is okay. That she is cared for. That her future is secure. We don't want any of Candace's money."

"But you are detectives for hire. Someone is paying you to find her. Is it the father?" Mother Alyssa shook her head disapprovingly. She stood and moved around until her bent neck put her face over ours, forcing us to peer upward at her. She pointed a finger, lamenting our client.

"And now you have found her. Should I expect that violent man, the man who destroyed this little girl's life, killed her mother, to show up on my doorstep since you have found us? Are you a harbinger of an evil wind?"

"No, the father will never know she is here. That is, if we are convinced she is safe and will be cared for. That you have not offered her sanctuary to get the money."

Sister Alyssa raised her eyebrows. "You are forthright. Are you accusing us of greed? You know we have taken a vow of poverty."

Roddy grinned. "I just did, yeah. Just being straight up. Can't lie to a nun, right?" He shrugged, not caring. "What's the deal with the moola, Sister?"

She smiled broadly, liking Roddy like everyone always did. "The moola, as you call it, is safe. Before the surgery, Candace—well, Elizabeth Vanner put the entire remaining 450,000 dollars into a trust. The fund in which it is invested pays a five percent return. The convent will receive the $20,000 dividend each year to raise the girl. She will live here and attend a local parochial school. When Sherri is ready for college, the head of the convent, with power of attorney, will help Sherri determine her educational needs and her college education will be paid out of the trust. Any remaining funds will be available to her once she graduates college or at age 26, whichever comes first. I will give you the name of the trust manager so you may verify this information is true. I trust you will keep it confidential?"

"Of course," Roddy said crisply with a tiny salute.

"Would you like to see her? If you do not mind, I will allow you to see her from a distance, but I would rather you did not speak to her. She is still confused and unsure of herself and her future. She keeps asking if she is going to be forced to leave here. I hope you understand."

Roddy nodded. He was now a fan of Sister Alyssa. The two decided they like the cut of the other's jib—whatever a jib was. I was simply along for the ride.

Sister Alyssa ever so slowly led us up a round spiral of

adobe stairs. We made it to the tower and looked over the beach area below. It would be nice if it were a fairy tale beach view, but it was not. The sky was menacing with rain. The shore was gravel strewn and the angry waves attacked the eroded beach. The rocky beach might suffice for a harbor for someone who'd been battered. From our vantage, we could clearly see the girl. Three of the younger nuns, all in their twenties, were with her and the four kicked a soccer ball around between them. We could see even from our distance that Sherri Vannick was all smiles. She was smaller than the others but was speedy and lithe. Once she got the ball away from the nuns and dribbled it into a natural alcove from the waves. She kicked the ball into a mound of boulders, her imaginary net, yelling "Goal," garnering laughs from her playmates and keepers. She danced with her arms spread in the air.

Sherri's face turned upward and she recognized Sister Alyssa in the distance at the building's zenith. She started to wave, but then saw the two men beside her. Her face, I could tell, clouded with concern for a moment, but Sister Alyssa smiled broadly and waved in an exaggerated way, letting the ten-year-old know all was fine in her world. I smiled too, realizing it was time to leave.

Late that afternoon, we returned downtown to the office. Roddy dropped me on the street while he drove his truck to the garage. I bought two coffees in the lobby. With two dark roasts in hand, I rode the elevator up, exited, set the coffees on the floor, fetched my key out of my pocket, and opened the door. I bent to retrieve the beverages. The elevator door rang. I heard the door open but didn't look up. I assumed it was Roddy.

"Java Jones at your service," I quipped. I gazed up. It was not Roddy. It was Calvin Grabber. And he was in a fury.

"You sent me up there to get me out of the way. Decoyed me and wasted my time. I finally figured it out." He pushed me back into the office, the coffee splashing onto the carpet as I dropped both cups. He chest-bumped me, and his thick thighs banging into my false leg and it buckled. I only stumbled for an instant. Calvin Grabber misinterpreted my sudden move. He grappled at the front of my shirt with both hands, and I stomped with my good foot on his instep. He howled with pain and toppled back into the desk. Grabber removed one hand from my shirt and grabbed the far edge of the desk for leverage. I used the advantage to force him back and further off balance.

Grabber drew back to punch me, one hand still on the desk for leverage, but suddenly Roddy was coming through the door. My partner waded into trouble as I knew he was born to do. With his big right paw, he grabbed the thick wrist of Grabber's which was still drawing back. Roddy, with his right hand like a vice on Grabber's wrist, forced his arm behind him until the man tucked at the waist. Grabber's face went down onto the desk. His left hand trailed over the edge. Roddy opened the drawer six inches and then slammed it hard. Hard as hell. Fingers lipped over the edge broke like kindling and Grabber screamed like something inhuman. The injured man yanked his hand free, but Roddy slammed two open palms into the Grabber's shoulders. The man, pain still registering in his face, fell backwards onto the floor in front of us. He was on his ass facing us. Grabber was momentarily surprised, not used to being outmuscled. Roddy used the instant to his advantage. He reached down into the second drawer of the desk and pulled a gun to the fore.

It was a huge silver-plated British Webley with a seven-inch barrel. The gun sight on the barrel was three-quarters of an inch high. Roddy slapped Grabber's face with the long barrel, grinding it and its sight into Grabber's face, cutting a long mean furrow that showed red along the man's left cheek. Grabber crumpled onto the floor.

"You broke all my fingers," Grabber whined, his good hand holding his damaged one like a drowned kitten.

"Jerk off with the other hand, you sick son-of-a-bitch. Your fingers are the least of your worries. I'm about to blow your fucking head off." Roddy was shaking with anger. The skin around his temples was purple and pulsing.

Grabber's pupils increased in size by approximately three times. "Why? For what? For grabbing your friend? I didn't even hit him. I was just trying to scare him enough so he would tell me where my wife and daughter are."

Roddy laughed and looked at me. "Grace here doesn't scare worth a damn. I've seen him run right at a whole building full of wild-eyed Baathists shooting AKs at him. You..." he slapped the gun barrel against Grabber's ear again, drawing blood. "You," he repeated. "You don't scare either of us. But that doesn't mean I'm not going to blow your fucking brains all over that wall behind you."

"Why? Why?"

"Because you beat her. You beat your wife bad. Candace ran from you and then you hired us to do your dirty work and find her. Your end game was for us to bring her home so you could beat her again. Or you didn't want her back. Maybe you just wanted that half a million of hers. And we took your money to find her. I'm ashamed." He slapped the gun barrel against Grabber's ear again. "And I don't like being ashamed of my behavior. I have a woman and a daughter in my life now and I'm trying to be a better man."

Grabber began to blubber. Roddy popped him hard with the gun against the crown of his skull this time. Blood dripped down from his hairline onto his white collar, creating a stark red stain.

Roddy put the barrel between Grabber's eyes and cocked the gun. It grew intensely quiet in the room. Grabber wet himself. "What can I do?"

Roddy laughed. "You mean besides buy adult diapers? Well, first you promise you're going to stop looking for your wife. We've verified Candace is someplace you'll never come close to finding. You will never come close to her. You try and find her, I kill you. You come after us, we got a band of brothers who will kill you. I will leave instructions and a sniper rifle to my whole mentally unstable army unit to take you off the board if anything happens to either Grace here or me. Got it?"

"Okay, okay. I don't even want Candace back, but my daughter. I need... I want..." he sobbed. "I want Sherri back. I love her."

I wanted to shout, "But you killed her mother, the person she loved most in life," but I did not. Roddy was currently perfect in his role of deranged bad cop. I remained silent.

Roddy paused, selecting his next words carefully. "I've looked over your accounting. I've seen your bank records. I know you have about three million liquid floating about in various banks. I also know you didn't pay taxes on it."

Grabber sneered, "So you're going to blackmail me by threatening an IRS action? That hardly would be as bad as the assault charges I could file on you."

Roddy dipped his chin toward me. "I got someone to testify you were assaulting him when I came into the office. Doesn't even need to be true, although it is. We'd embellish. No, I don't give a shit about your little tax loophole hideaways. I care about your daughter's future."

Grabber narrowed his eyes at Roddy. He still held his damaged hand gingerly. It trembled as he clinched it to his chest. "I care about my daughter much more than you."

"Your behavior to the contrary," Roddy smirked. "I'm going to let you prove it to me. You're going to leave here, go to the emergency room and get your hand fixed. You're going to tell the doctors that you closed your fingers in your car door. Make sure you stick to that story because I will check."

"Okay, and then what?" Grabber's eyes had regained a little balance. He was still crying, but now it might have been shame, but the shame was in being bested by Roddy, not what he had done to his wife. It made me sick.

"Then you're going to take the information I'm going to give you. There's a bank official in downtown Santa Barbara. You're going to tell that bank official to put a cool million tomorrow into a blind trust to go to your daughter upon her

26th birthday. I will make sure Candace knows you've done so with the best of intentions. You are bidding them farewell and wishing them well. You are giving a million bucks to your little girl to make sure she is well cared for. Her mother's money will certainly be enough to get them through until Sherri is an adult."

Grabber shook his head no. "I need to see her. She's my little girl."

Roddy took the Webley sighted barrel and rammed it roughly into Grabber's nose. It began to bleed down his face and into his mouth. He began to sob again. "Okay, okay, I'll do it." His words were indistinct with the blood in his mouth and gun barrel stuck in his nostril.

"Any variation, you end up with a pie plate sized hole out the back of your head. We got a deal?"

"Yes." Grabber dropped his gaze to the floor, a defeated and crushed man.

Roddy drew the barrel back out of Grabber's nose, carving yet another channel. "Then get out of here. And you should know, I bugged every one of your electronic devices when I was at your house. You so much as think of calling the cops or anyone else and we'll know, so don't even try. And even if you would get us—though you're not man enough—but if you did, it wouldn't matter. You would be dead before dark the day you did us in. We have very violent friends."

Grabber staggered to his feet. He grabbed the door handle with his good hand.

"Grabber?" Roddy called to the man with blood mixing with tears across his smeared face. "You have until the end of business tomorrow to deposit the money into the trust. Before 5:00 pm. If you don't do it, I'm hunting you by dark."

Grabber nodded and stumbled out the door.

When the door closed, Roddy switched off his act. He turned to me and smiled with a sorrowful look. "Almost five o'clock here, buddy. We got nothing to do for 24 hours. What do you say we drive up to Monro Bay in the morning and donate the ten grand Grabber paid us to the convent? Can't really keep it, right?"

I was stunned at Roddy's change in mood—the rage turning to pleasantry in but a second—but decided to go with it. "Sure, there's a good barbeque place in Santa Barbara. Wanna keep enough cash out to buy side of ribs for both of us? Really tie one on after we take the check to Sister Alyssa?"

"Nah, let's give her the whole enchilada. Ribs are on me." Roddy beamed at me as he put his gun back in the holster.

"You know we're letting Grabber walk on a murder, although he doesn't even know his wife is dead, but he killed her," I said.

"Yeah," Roddy answered, "but if we filed on him, then the whole Brand New Me gang goes to prison. They are saving lives. I can't do it. How 'bout you?"

"Nope," I replied, "me neither. Hey Rod, that Webley didn't even have a round in the chamber when you cocked it, did it?" I laughed.

"Nah," he acknowledged. "I need to have work done on it. Just left in the desk until I have time to take to a gunsmith." He ran his hand along the weapon's site, which glistened with a drop of blood.

"Ouch," I said. "You know, when you stuck it in his nose all I could think of was the scene when Roman Polanski cuts Jack Nicholson's nose in Chinatown."

"Me too, man. Me too." We both laughed.

"What you gonna do tonight, Roddy?"

"I got two ladies training me to be a better man tonight. How about you?"

"Coyote and me having burgers off the grill. Wanna trade?"

"Not a chance, Gracer. Not a chance in the world."

FRIENDS WITH BENEFITS

"First of all, don't judge me," the client said.

Roddy said, "We won't." Then he stood and added, "Excuse me while I stretch my legs."

I had to smile as my partner in the detective agency stood and arched his massive frame, moving his legs in a balancing act reminiscent of a more graceful Frankenstein monster. See, Roddy lost his legs in Iraq to an IED. If he were stretching them now, he'd be bending titanium prosthetics.

I frowned at him to sit down and behave. Roddy smiled back, but he complied. The client acted a bit confused, but she was so gorgeous—a tall, curvy, spiked-hair brunette— that she could act however she wanted.

"Most people who hire a private detective aren't usually revealing their best behavior, Ms. Rybolt," I said calmly. Getting clients to disclose information was a normal part of the gig. Usually their problems were embarrassing, but nothing we hadn't heard before – and certainly we'd heard worse than most revealed. I couldn't imagine this woman's actions were bad enough to move the scale of dirty deeds we'd learned to a new high—or low.

"I'm a nymphomaniac," the woman said. "A sex addict, plain and simple. I have sex ten to twelve times a week."

Roddy laughed politely and said, "Damn, lady. Where were you when I was single?"

I gave him a stern look and started to apologize, "Ms. Rybolt, I am so..."

She interrupted. "Call me Tasha. And I'm not offended."

The tension in the room turned down a notch. The woman took a sip of her coffee and began to explain what she needed us to do. Her story did not take long.

Tasha was in sales—corporate sales of computer software. Her company was marketing a new proprietary software. Right now, she was promoting a new program called Collide-a-scope, a simulator that could measure the changes in chemical compounds out in parts per million without having to create samples and test them in a laboratory. It was cutting edge stuff, she said.

Roddy commented that it sounded like the program might save the lives of millions of animals currently used in product testing.

"Exactly," Tasha said, leaning forward in her chair. "And think about drug trials involving humans as well. It could save millions of dollars on those kind of tests. Drugs could get to market sooner, saving thousands of lives."

"And how does your sexual predilection impact this program?" I asked.

"I'm also a workaholic, work 60 hours a week. That doesn't

leave time for relationships, so I tend to have sexual relation-ships with my vendors. I was in Los Angeles last week showing a prototype of the program to three companies. Each one has a young attractive point person. I met each of them at their homes. We had sex, enthusiastic sex, and when I orgasm, I faint." Tasha paused, waiting for our reaction. Then she added, "I always do."

I did not speak and hoped Roddy wouldn't crack wise. He didn't and demurely took a swig of coffee, barely opening his mouth. I thought his right eyebrow had a noticeable tic, but I wasn't sure. I couldn't wait to hear his review after she left. I was sure he was working on his comedy bit right now.

"Only for about five or ten minutes," she said, "I mean, when I pass out."

I nodded. Roddy continued to be impassive, but then after a long pause, he seemed to ignite with the significance of Tasha's revelation.

Roddy stated his insight aloud. "And one of them, while you were zonked, stole the program?"

"Yes, from the flash drive I had in my purse," she said. "The next day I received a message demanding $300,000 from me personally to get it back."

"Seems like kind a small amount for a program so valuable."

Tasha nodded. "My company does not know somebody took the program from me. They certainly don't know how I lost the program. The only good news is the demo I showed that day is currently encrypted with a key lock. The actual program won't work without the encryption key loaded on Collide-a-Scope."

"They want 300 K to give the demo back and not tell your boss about your hanky-panky?" Roddy paraphrased.

Tasha nodded. "Paying would wipe me out, my 401K, everything. And then I don't know that they wouldn't keep a copy anyway. It's terribly upsetting." Her face clouded up. Tears rimmed in her eyes. I watched carefully but wasn't sure of the true emotion here. It seemed like there was something bigger she wasn't telling us.

Tasha then filled in the gaps in her tale. She told us about each of the vendors she'd slept with—A, B, and C, or as Roddy later named them: Atta, Boy, and Cupid. She'd known all of them for a year. She had slept with each of them numerous times before. Tasha thought of them as friends. Friends with benefits. She considered none of them to be serious lovers. She had no idea which one had stolen the program. The blackmail note had arrived by email from a Stockholm email server exchange. She was to send the money to a numbered account in Cyprus. It was all anonymous and well planned. The trail erased itself afterwards too. Programmers were good blackmailers.

Roddy spent an hour with Tasha on his computer. They checked the email IP address, the routing instructions on the banking account, the flash drive that held the program. All netted no new intel.

"What can you do to help me?" Tasha said in frustration and fury after Roddy hit another dead-end.

Roddy, all shoulders in his white oxford shirt and knit tie, shuffled across the room, his unlaced tennies scraping across the carpet. "I got an idea," he said. "Can you get a full version of the program? Not just a demo. Something we could use as bait?"

Tasha furrowed her eyebrows for a moment, but then said yes.

"There are flash drives out there with their own power source, an internal battery," Roddy said. "I could install a program on three drives that would send out a beacon, a Bluetooth transmission when someone accessed the drive. It would not travel far, but if someone were right outside the house with a computer tracking the signal, we'd know as soon as someone put the drive into a computer, attempting to copy the contents."

Tasha said, "Which means I'd have to go back and visit each client and give him a chance to take my flash drive and download the information from it again."

I raised my eyebrows. "Which means having sex with each of them again, knowing one of them is a blackmailer. It could be dangerous."

Tasha Rybolt stood up and shrugged. "As a nympho, I guess I'll have to take one for the team."

Roddy smiled. "Three, actually."

The scam was this—Tasha was to get the full unencrypted program on a flash drive—something she was not supposed to have access to, but she thought she could get. She would head back to corporate in San Francisco, steal a copy of the unencrypted program, and return in two days. Then Tasha would reschedule with each of her contacts, saying she had the complete program this time. We hoped a full version of Collide-a-Scope would be enough temptation for our black-mailer to risk downloading the program during Ms. Rybolt's post-coital bliss. Roddy would be outside in his truck with a laptop equipped with a signal tracker to grab the beacon and verify who the blackmailer was.

When Tasha arrived back at our office on Wednesday with the stolen software, she left messages for each of her three customers for the second time in as many weeks. While she worked the phones, Roddy loaded the software with the key onto his special flash drives. He also loaded a hidden program with the beacon Bluetooth program on each drive. At the last moment, he decided each flash drive needed one more thing.

"What's that?" I asked.

"A computer virus. It's a variation of the old Klez virus of 2001. That one infected computers and replicated itself by sending emails to other people in the computer's contact files. It was a tremendously effective destroyer, but clumsy in that it required an email to migrate. This worm destroys data just like that one, but it's particularly nasty in that it's suicidal."

"I don't understand."

"It doesn't attempt to replicate," Roddy said. "It just kills everything in the host hard drive. Melts all the files into sludge. This version is called Ophelia-K and it destroys all portal input commands first, so the user is locked out. Then it takes all the files in reverse chronological order and destroys them by randomizing all data and then corrupting it. It's a nasty fucker."

"If our blackmailer has not saved the program off the computer and then uploads the new Collide-a-Scope onto the same hard drive, he'll lose everything he stole from Tasha?"

"Yeah, along with everything else on the computer. I hope he loses his porn collection," Roddy snarled. Then he looked over to Tasha. "No offense."

She smiled. "None taken."

After the drives were ready, Tasha scheduled appointments with each of the buyers for the next afternoon and evening. She was flirty on the phone and seemed to put aside any worries she had about sleeping with a blackmailer as she agreed on a time to meet each man. We listened in on the calls. Atta, Boy, and Cupid all seemed enthusiastic to see her again. I looked at Tasha and completely understood their enthusiasm.

Roddy and I accompanied Tasha to dinner that night. Karen, Roddy's lady, joined us. We went to Otium, which is on Hope Street downtown next to the Broad Museum. Karen hadn't been out to dinner much since little Gracie had been born and she'd been wanting to go to this place. Karen looked amazing for having just had a baby three months prior. Plus, Roddy had told her his new client was a nympho—so Karen tried a little more than normal to look fantastic. Karen trusted Roddy, but knowing your man is working with a nympho is a worry. Karen was determined to keep Tasha's hands (and legs) off Roddy. In fact, Karen seemed to be pushing Tasha at me all evening. I wasn't having any of it. Sleeping with clients was not working for me these days. My bad trip with Angie, the magician's assistant, had been my one and done.

Nonetheless, Karen clung to Roddy a little that evening. And more than one guy in the room checked out Roddy's lady love. Her body type, already lean after the pregnancy, was completely different than Tasha. Tasha was all bust, hips, and long legs. Karen was tiny by those standards, but her face and eyes were exquisite, and her hair perfect, black, and wavy. Roddy and I definitely had the two most beautiful women in the restaurant at our table. It was a great evening. The food good, the company great, and Tasha seemed grateful for our companionship prior to her mission of the next day. Roddy winked at me as I volunteered to take Tasha back to her hotel, but I offered no advances and she was all lady as I left her at the hotel entrance.

In the morning, Roddy and Tasha met me at the office. He wired her purse with a communications device that allowed him to hear conversations within about 20 feet. They established a safe word of "Back off." If she said those two words, Roddy was going to bust the door in and come in with weapon drawn. Tasha understood it was a last resort to go that route. Then he gave her one of the drives. He would keep the other two until she needed one. No sense in having the potential blackmailer find three drives in her purse.

I did not go with them. My day was different than theirs.

Well, I too was getting screwed. I was meeting with our accountant and paying our quarterly taxes to the federal government. Afterwards, I was having dinner with Bob Lee, our biggest client, who was in town. We met about every other month and he had called earlier. Lee ran Welmar Industries which kept us on retainer. It was the account that kept the lights on some months. When Bob called and wanted to talk, I talked. So, I was out of pocket until after dinner, which in L.A. meant at least 9:30. Our plan was to meet at Sundowners, an afterhours gambling place disguised as a steak, eggs, and bourbon bar just outside of Pacific Palisades, at 10 p.m.

"Well," I said that night, sliding into the black leather booth at the back of the restaurant, "where's Tasha?"

"Powdering her nose," Roddy answered.

"Any luck?"

"Too much."

"How so?"

"All three of them downloaded the flash drive. Melted their hard drives." With those words, Roddy pounded his drink and waved our barmaid over to take my order and bring him another. "All three confronted her when they loaded the drive, melted down the computer. Totally busted but still bitching at her. She got in a yelling match with each of them. She called out 'Back off' once and I kicked in a door. It was not exactly a banner day."

"You're telling me all three of them were blackmailing her?" I asked, incredulous.

"No, but all three downloaded the flash drive contents after the bedroom party concluded."

"So, which one is the blackmailer?"

"Don't know," Roddy said, shaking his head. "Just know all three of Tasha's friends with benefits took unfair advantage. By the way," he said, taking a slug of the bourbon in the new highball glass set before him, "putting a com device in Tasha's purse was a bad idea. She told us she faints after sex, right?"

"Right."

"She just didn't tell us how long it takes that to happen. We scheduled her, ahem, appointments three hours apart. With traffic considerations, we were late to the last two."

"Lots of moaning, eh?" I asked, laughing.

"Like listening to Donna Summers' 'Love to Love You, Baby' for nine hours straight."

I laughed. Tasha was approaching across the sparsely populated restaurant. At this time of night, all the action at this place took place behind the mahogany walls at the gaming tables. I imagined our buddy Rat was at the poker table right now. Tasha joined us, sitting next to me.

"I guess we learned all three of your clients are rats," I said, trying to be consolatory.

Tasha nodded glumly.

"And all are in need of new computers," Roddy added.

"And one needs a front door," Tasha added.

"So, what's our next step?" I asked.

Tasha looked at the two of us. "I'm afraid that is out of my hands now. The blackmailer has contacted my employer. My boss just called and told me to 'get my ass' back to San Francisco. I lost the territory, so I'm afraid I won't be back to Los Angeles for a while. You've been so nice. I'm sorry." Tasha grasped her wine glass and I noticed the tremor in her hand. I thought I detected fear in her voice and demeanor.

Tasha's news was a real downer and she asked to be returned to her hotel room. It had been a difficult day. We left the restaurant without eating.

I met Roddy at the office in the morning. He had a wild-eyed stare that told me he was on some kind of stimulant and had been up all night.

I handed him a coffee. "What's the story, morning glory? You got that look."

"Yeah," Roddy said, "I smelled a rat after Tasha got that call last night. And I was right. We've been played for patsies."

"How? What's going on?"

"Well, the Collide-a-Scope is a stolen program. It was stolen from a chemical laboratory in London about two years ago. It was designed for the functions we discussed with Tasha, but she was peddling it to pot dealers, boutique dealers. It can tell them down to a millionth of a gram how much of one type of weed vs. another into a variety for a perfect high. You know, blended varietals, just like wine. Boutique pot for the Laurel Canyon crowd."

"Oh lovely, and we fried the computers of three different

drug dealers."

Roddy shrugged. "That's not even close to the worse part. The program was stolen from the London lab by the Russian mafia. Tasha is in sales for the Moscow mob. They are trying to muscle in on L.A.'s pot trade."

"And now her handlers have found out she stole the program and may have lost it to L.A.'s drug trade without proper compensation."

"A-huh," Roddy said, "and, Tasha's last name isn't Rybolt. It's Rybolovleva. And I checked her itinerary. She didn't fly back to San Francisco this morning. She flew to New York, connecting to Rome."

"In the wind."

"Yep."

"So, we're out two days' pay, plus whatever the flash drives cost, plus any random expenses."

"I bought the virus off the dark web for a grand."

"Lovely. We're out like $3,500. Damn, I just saw the accountant yesterday. Remind me to deduct that grand expense in three months when I pay the quarterlies again."

"Going to be hard to expense a grand spent on a computer virus purchased on the dark web."

I looked at Roddy, "You're saying you didn't get a receipt?"

He just laughed.

And then the phone rang. Roddy hit the speaker button.

The man on the phone said his name was Boris.

Roddy asked, "Where are Moose and Squirrel?"

Boris did not laugh. Instead, he said he worked in San Francisco in the importing business. One of his employees had not shown up for work this morning, a Ms. Natasha Rybolovleva. Since she was AWOL, he'd checked her company phone records. Her phone, paid for by him, was now not working, but over the last few days had made several calls to this number. She had resigned by email, but still had an item that belonged to Boris's firm—an expensive item. It was important he come down and discuss the issue with us. He would be here at our office at seven this evening. Could we arrange to be available at that time? He wouldn't accept no as an answer. We scheduled the appointment. I hung up, ending the call.

"How do you want to manage it?" Roddy asked.

"I think we plan a reception," I said. "Let's get to work."

Boris arrived ten minutes late, but it didn't matter. We were ready. He entered our office with two—and there is no other word to use than this one—henchmen. Both men were all muscle, built of solid Russian stock. They wore dark suits and each lumberjack-sized bodyguard had a large bulge under his left arm. I was guessing .45 calibers.

Bossman Boris was also a big man. His face was white, whiter than it should have been and it was also shiny and emotionless. I recognized the extensive plastic surgery which had left that look, a lack of empathy. It was a sociopath's face. Rearranged by a surgeon, but still a sociopath's face.

He looked as if he could step on a puppy and not mind.

His suit was black, his tie white with tiny black roses on it. His shirt was a deep, deep gray. He was perhaps 45 years old and his hair matched his shirt color. His lips were stretched tight across his shiny face. Finally, those lips moved.

"My name is Boris. We spoke earlier. Thank you for arranging to be here after your normal hours."

"No problem," I said. "I'm not sure private detectives have normal hours."

Roddy and I were both leaning against the credenza in the lobby. We stood, introduced ourselves and shook hands with "Boris." He gave no last name and his first was so stereotypical to be a joke. His grip was no joke, though. It was firm and his hands were as cold as his heart. The mobster made no apologies for not introducing his friends.

Roddy waved Boris toward my office door, which was closed. "Shall we?" he said.

The first henchman moved to the door in advance of his boss. Roddy opened the door. The big Russian stepped through but pulled up short when he saw the five people sitting in the room. He looked quizzically back at his boss who stepped forward and peered into the room.

"What is the meaning of this? Who are these people?"

I stepped into the room. "Let me introduce the other people joining our meeting. First up, this is Captain Janelle Jackson of the LAPD, and her assistant Detective First Class Speedy Khuzaymah."

The two stood. Janelle was as tall as Speedy in her heels, although he wore a straw fedora. Her face was friendly and intimidating at the same time. I had never understood how she did that. Speedy just looked intimidating. They were both black, Speedy darker. Both were thin and wore tight fitting suits. Their weapons showed on their hips, their badges on their lapels. Boris did not look pleased.

Then I introduced Atta, Boy, and Cupid, using their real names. I explained the relationship to the Russians. The cops already knew. "These three each downloaded proprietary software onto their personal computers yesterday to steal software to enhance their marijuana distribution businesses. Unfortunately, Roddy loaded the program with a computer virus. All three lost their computers, but we don't know if they still have the program on another device."

"And the program belongs to Boris here?" Janelle asked, liking the Agatha Christie set-up of this final scene.

"No," Roddy replied. "It belongs to a firm in London. It was stolen about a year ago. It was reported to Scotland Yard at that time and has since been reported in *Wired Magazine*."

Boris decided to get with the whole PBS British mystery theme of the party. He smiled, moved to my sideboard, and poured himself two fingers of scotch. He sat in the leather chair in front of my desk. "No, the program is not mine. I am here because my employee attempted to sell something to these three men. She attempted to make them believe my company was selling this stolen software. That is not the case, I assure you. She was working either on her own or on someone else's behalf."

Janelle smiled. "We'll see about that." She looked at me. "And who and where is this employee?"

I answered that one. "Ms. Natasha Rybolovleva is, I would think, halfway to Algiers by now. Boris said something to her last night on the phone that scared the hell out of her."

"Smart girl. She was hanging with the wrong crowd."

I nodded. Captain Jackson motioned to Roddy and Speedy. "Will you two please remove the weapons from Tweddle Dee and Tweddle Dum over there?"

Roddy held his exceptionally large Israeli Desert Eagle on the two men. Speedy took their firearms and dropped them in his side pockets. Speedy patted them down but found no more guns.

"We'll be checking your conceal-and-carry permits in a minute or two," Captain Jackson said. "Now for you." She motioned to Boris. "You packing?"

Boris shook his head no.

"You understand Detective Khuzaymah will have to check." Boris stood and put his hands up. Speedy patted him down. The Russian did not have a gun.

She looked at Boris' white shiny face. "We've already checked those three." She indicated the very nervous-looking pot dealers sitting in folding chairs in a semi-circle around her. Janelle was now holding court. "They didn't carry any weapons in here. Pot dealers don't like guns as much as gangsters," she said reflectively.

"Let's handle things one at a time," Janelle said. "Clayton, how much does Boris' firm owe you?"

"$3,500."

"Do you take credit cards?"

"Sure."

Janelle nodded at Boris. "I'm sure you'd like to take care of that bill right now. Am I right?"

Boris, who was again reclining in his chair, reached ever

so slowly into his suit pocket and removed a slim wallet. He handed me an American Express card.

"Sorry," I said, "Only take Visa, MasterCard, and Discover."

Speedy laughed and Boris took back the Amex card and handed me a Visa. I ran the charge.

"Gave you one percent discount for quick pay. Saved you thirty-five bucks," I said, handing him his card.

Boris nodded with a grim smile. We were not going to be friends. No repeat business this time, I was afraid.

"Now for the three stooges here," Janelle said, turning to address the dealers. "Do any of you still have a copy of the computer program called Collide-a-Scope in your possession?"

All three swore they did not.

"We'll be checking. I've passed your names on to Vice. The information we gave them was sufficient to get a warrant. They are in the process of serving those warrants. I'm afraid your residences are going to be quite messy when you get home. I hope you were wise enough to keep your marijuana business separate from your home. If Vice finds evidence of your dealings there, they could impound the property. I understand from Roddy here that you all live in beautiful homes. It would be a shame for them to end up at auction."

Janelle turned to Boris. "Unless you have a claim against these three, I'm going to allow them to go. Although," she said, "I don't imagine they will be running around free for long. Which might be for their own good since they've crossed the Russian mob. Maybe a little protective jail time is a good thing for them."

Boris shrugged. "I have no idea what you're talking about. My business in San Francisco is legitimate. I sell computer security. Some software. I import. I dabble."

"I'm sure you do," Janelle said, smiling. "But I don't want to hear about these three ending up in Catalina Bay. Is that clear?"

Boris nodded.

Janelle repeated, "Is that clear?" Her voice rose a register.

"Yes," he said. "It is clear."

She turned to the three dealers. "Then you may go."

It did not take them long to exit my office, the foyer, and the building.

"And what to do about you," pondered Janelle. "Roddy, what do you think we should do with them? I mean, we believe they threatened the life of a young woman last night, that they stole a software program in England last year, or at least acquired it from someone who did, and we think they are in the drug trade, probably smuggling heroin or other drugs into the port, using their import/export business as a cover."

"None of which you can prove and none of which is in your jurisdiction," said Boris.

Janelle shrugged. "True, but we have probable cause to take you all downtown to run prints, check the firearms for proper permits, and to validate your identification. Maybe we'll even contact Interpol and the FBI about the stolen software while we have you downtown. There might even be international warrants issued on you. I'm feeling lucky." Janelle smiled. "I hope you have fresh undies on. You know I can hold you for 24 hours before having to charge you or kick you free."

Boris nodded. "And I get to call an attorney."

"True, but I'm going to jam up your schedule until I turn you over to the feds about 23 hours from now," she replied. "Speedy, you want to call central? Have a paddy wagon brought around. We have three passengers. Bigguns, you tell 'em."

Janelle turned to me. "Anything else you need, Clayton? I got to say, this is the first time you handled things the right way, calling us in like you did. Though I can't imagine why. Keep up the good work. You got anything else?"

I looked at Boris. "You want your printed receipt by mail or is email okay?"

He called me a bad word. Speedy reached out and banged Boris' head against the wall. "Not in front of the lady," he said, and then applied the cuffs.

FIENDS WITH BENEFITS

"First of all, please don't judge me," the woman said.

"We've been hearing that a lot lately," Roddy responded with a slight smirk that the woman did not register. She sat there in a frumpy skirt bunched around her waist like she was still wearing a larger size after losing significant weight. Her face was fleshy with full lips. Her hair was light brown and curled around her face in natural ringlets, like she was of Mediterranean descent. It was a good face, but a severe one, joyless somehow. Her complexion was fair and freckles were evident across the bridge of her nose. She sat primly with her legs uncrossed, tightly together and pale below the navy skirt. Her name was Naomi Wright.

"What my partner means," I interjected, "is that most of our clients come to us with delicate problems."

Roddy nodded, "Yeah, that's what I meant."

Now I gave him the look. He settled down, cutting the smart ass quotient by at least half.

"My problem is delicate. You see I was raped two months ago."

That stopped both Roddy and me. We exchanged looks.

"I'm sorry. That's just terrible," I said. Roddy nodded in agreement. "However, something like that should be reported to the police. Have you done so?"

"No."

"Why have you waited? Two months is a long time. It will be difficult to find the individual responsible..." I trailed off as she waved my words away.

"My assailant inadvertently dropped his wallet at the scene. Afterward, as he dressed, you know. I have his name. I've already tracked him down."

I leaned back in my chair. "I'm afraid I don't understand what you want us to do."

Naomi Wright leaned forward. "As I said, this is quite a delicate thing. A man broke in my apartment and raped me. I am single and I must admit that despite being in my mid-30's I have had very few relationships with men." She paused. "That might make it sound like I prefer women. I do not. I am heterosexual."

"Okay," I said.

"During the rape, and this is the part that is so taboo I hesitate to tell it, but here it goes. I found the act enjoyable. I know that even saying those words is sick and disturbed, but the man was actually quite gentle. I was terribly frightened, but he was not violent. He held a gun on me at first. Then it turned into, well, it turned into something else. It was so exciting, so forbidden. I have had few sexual encounters, but

I will say, this was the best I have experienced. I know it is strange. And taboo. Wrong."

Roddy shook his head as he stood, taking it in, but bothered by the admission. It was out-of-bounds. He refilled our coffee cups. When he sat back down, she continued.

"And after he left, I felt so ashamed," the woman said. "I mean, to experience orgasm for the first time with a rapist. I mean, that's just unacceptable. Right?"

"And then you found his wallet? On the floor afterwards?" I asked, prodding toward what I hoped was less tenuous ground.

"Yes, I did. I pondered what to do. Should I call the police? Should I contact him directly? I waited over a week, wondering what to do."

"And after a week?"

"I went and purchased a firearm. A Glock nine-millimeter. A small gun, really, with a ten-shot magazine."

Roddy spoke this time. "We're familiar with the weapon. What did you do after getting the weapon?"

"I practiced with it for a few days," she said, and now her voice trailed away.

I thought the worse. "And you've killed him?"

"Oh no," Naomi Wright said. "I did go to his apartment. It was late and his apartment is not in a particularly good part of town. Culver City and in a rundown section at that."

"Did you encounter the man?"

"Yes. His name is Samson Henderson."

"How did you get in? Did you ring the bell? Knock on the door?"

"No, surprisingly his door was unlocked. It was late—between two and three in the morning."

"Okay, and was he awake?"

"Oh, no. It was like when he accosted me. He was in bed asleep."

Roddy exclaimed, "What happened?"

"I raped him back."

I set down my mug before I dropped it. "You did what?"

"I raped him back. I held the gun against his head and said his name. He woke with a start and I told him not to move or I'd kill him. Then I told him that turnabout was fair play. I had planned what I was going to do so I was in a dress. I wore no underpants and I climbed on and made him have sex with me. It was magnificent."

"Umm, Ms. Wright," I said, "you've just admitted to a felony in front of licensed private detectives. Technically we're supposed to inform law enforcement when that happens."

"Oh, that's just talk. I've read about you two. You're not going to call the police."

Roddy shrugged. "That's true. We're not." He looked at me and then back to Naomi Wright. "What happened next?" he asked.

"Oh, we went back and forth for about five weeks then. Twice a week, he would sneak into my apartment late at night and we would do all sorts of things. Sometimes at his place, sometimes at mine. I've had quite an initiation."

Roddy pursed his lips. "Different strokes, I suppose."

I nodded. "And what would you hire us to do after two months of mutually agreed upon sexual imposition?"

"Yes, it's tawdry, I know. I need you to find Sam. He's missing. He didn't show up for our Tuesday 'date' at my place. I thought he overslept and I tried to call the next morning, but his cell was disconnected or something. I went to his apartment last night. I have a key now. His apartment was empty. He's disappeared."

"You want to hire us in a missing person's case?"

"Exactly. I need you to find my Sam."

I looked at Roddy. "You game?

He looked back wryly. "What the hell."

After the client had left, I spoke to Roddy with disgust. "What are we going to do when we find this asshole?"

"You mean, you've also considered the fact that most rapists are not single victim perpetrators?"

"Yes," I said. "He's probably raped other women. In fact, he may have a rap sheet or he may not be in the apartment anymore because he's in custody."

Roddy nodded. "That's our first check."

Indeed, Samson Henderson had a record, but not for rape. He was a B & E artist. A two-time loser on burglary. Had done one year in county his first time. Then a nickel in the State Penitentiary at Corcoran. However, Sammy Boy had no rape charges pending against him. He was not currently in custody. He *was* on probation.

Roddy and I went to see Henderson's probation officer. She was typical of what I remembered about a P.O. from my days on the force—overworked and extremely devoted, but so worn down by the system to be demoralized and no longer looking for trouble. Getting through a day was a win for this woman.

"Ms. Simons?" Roddy said, sticking his head inside the cracked office door of a basement office in the county courthouse.

"Yes, I'm Greta Simons. What can I do for you?"

We introduced ourselves. "We're looking for one of your guys. A Mister Samson Henderson."

"What's he done?"

"Nothing criminal," I lied. "It's a family thing. His folks want to know what happened to him. They've lost contact."

She raised her eyebrows, not really believing us, but glad our visit was not going to mess up her already booked-to-the-gills, drowning-in-paperwork day.

"And you need a current address?"

"Exactly."

"I'm not supposed to, but I'll give it to you. With a caveat."

"What's that?"

"Don't contact me if he doesn't live there."

The address Sam Henderson's P.O. gave us was not the same address as the apartment where Naomi Wright had been meeting him. But it didn't matter. He did not reside at either these days.

Time to move on to step two. Hack him.

This was a multi-step process. Phone records, banking records – Visa or MasterCard charges. Registration on a vehicle, parking tickets issued and their location. Pay stubs with FICA payments and state taxes taken out. It is easy to find employers and if the perp was still going to the job.

Roddy struggled with Sammy Boy's digital footprint. Our rapist boyfriend was living off the grid. No phone. The number Naomi had was no longer working and was a burner prepaid at that. There were no credit cards currently in his name. There were numerous delinquent accounts with old addresses—all prior to his state time served. His vehicle, a '66 VW bug, was a beater – but with licensed tags registered to the old address. Sammy was in the wind.

Sam's parking tickets were many and varied in their distribution. There was no centralized address for the location of the given tickets. No clues. Roddy said running down the tickets wasn't worth our time. Especially because we found Sammy did have an employer. He worked at a carwash and detailing place in Lucerne-Higuera just south of the Culver City Junction near Ince Blvd. and Lindblade. It was less than a half hour away.

Roddy and I went there, and by Naomi's description and a discreet fiver to a black co-worker with a bad limp, we verified Sam Henderson was at work. With a clean car freshly detailed and vacuumed, we watched the car wash from the parking lot of an In-N-Out Burger joint until closing time. Sam got in his VW, drove to a liquor store, bought a sixer, and then purchased TV dinners at a corner market. We followed Henderson from there to an apartment complex, close to his old one. The new apartment was right off the Hawthorne 105 in Lennox. Henderson was an oblivious driver and we were able to follow him very easily. We pulled up across the street from the complex and watched as Henderson used a key to check his mailbox.

Roddy is a noticeable guy with his size and his double amputee/prosthesis limp, so I followed Henderson into his building. I got to the lobby in time to see him, but I didn't get on the elevator as he pressed four.

After the elevator door closed, I humped it up the stairs, but missed which apartment he entered, but it was in the southern block of the floor, which narrowed it to four doors. Roddy and I got him on the first try, calling out "Pizza delivery" with our knock.

Henderson opened his door with no chain or peep hole glance. Just opened it wide. Roddy showed him a weapon in a holster. I quickly flipped a fake badge at him, not giving him time to read it. Our perp rolled his eyes and stepped to the side, letting us in.

"You from the parole board? I know I got a bad address on the form. I've only been here two days. Haven't had a day off when the P.O. offices were open that I could get down there to do the paperwork."

Roddy waved him off. "Sit down. We're here for Naomi Wright."

Henderson swore. "What does that crazy bitch want? I moved to get away from her."

I nodded. "Her story of impending nuptials was exaggerated?"

Henderson, who was a blocky man with the beginning of a beer belly, looked at me dumbly. "What does that mean?"

Roddy said, "It means she thought your sick little game was true love."

Henderson moaned. "Naomi just didn't get it. She was nice enough. Willing certainly. Surprisingly good cook too, although I only had breakfast at her place a couple of times after."

The word 'after' stuck in my craw. "What do you mean she just didn't get it?" I asked.

Henderson got serious. "Look, I like her. But pretend rape isn't rape. That's not what I need. I know I'm messed up inside. I..." He paused, choosing his words carefully. "I get off on different stuff than she does."

"You need the danger to be real. The fear of the victim to be real," I asked, rhetorically.

"Yeah, Naomi is a nice woman. I like her but liking her ruined it for me."

Roddy looked sick. "You moved away to ditch her? To move on to greener pastures."

"Yeah," Henderson said, thinking incorrectly this conversation was going well. "I didn't want her to get hurt. I care about her."

"Which leaves us with a problem," I said. "Do you plan to rape again?"

"No," Henderson said, shaking his head unconvincingly. "I learned my lesson. I'm just going to use porn. I know I got a problem."

"And you've made it ours," Roddy said.

"What do you mean?" Henderson asked. He honestly

thought we were going to leave and let him hurt someone else.

"What my partner means is we don't believe you." I said. "Have you raped anyone since you moved?"

"Hell no, it's only been two days."

"Wrong answer," Roddy said. "It's only been two days. You just haven't had time in your busy schedule?"

Henderson said, "No, that's not what I meant." He waited for a long moment. "What are you guys going to do? Hey," he said, with a sudden realization. "You guys aren't even real cops."

"I don't know what we're going to do," I said, standing. "But keep your dick in your pants and we'll be in touch."

As we left. Roddy looked at me. "Did you just use the words 'dick' and 'touch' in the same sentence to that freak?" He smirked.

"Shut up. When we get to the car, let's call Speedy."

Speedy Khuzaymah was an LAPD detective. He answered on the first ring, saying his name. He was not known for his conversational skills.

"Speed, it's Grace."

"How's my favorite peeper?"

"Need a favor."

"Color my African skin a new shade of surprised."

"Holy shrine, Speedy," I said. "Did you just make a joke, one with racial overtones? 'Cause that's unlike you."

"I woke up on the right side of my prayer mat."

"Damn, that's two."

He laughed on his end of the line. "What do you need? I'm busy."

"Roddy and I ran across a guy on a case. He seems hinky. Like rapist hinky."

"Rapist is beyond hinky."

"Yeah, and he's got a rap sheet for B & E. It would be handy if he's wanted on something."

"Give me the particulars."

I did.

Speedy called back first thing in the morning.

"What you got?" I said, my phone on speaker as I drove down from Topanga.

"Nothing open on him. No crimes being investigated where his prints or description are possibilities. Hinky, yes. Wanted right now, no. Except I talked to his P.O. Woman named Greta Simons. She said you promised to call her if Henderson wasn't where he was listed with the Dept. of Corrections. She said he came in this morning and filed a change of address form. All in proper order. Unusual for one of her guys to follow the rules. Said to thank you."

"Meaning you can't violate him."

"Not now," the police detective responded. "What's going on with this guy?"

"Not enough to put him back in jail, I'm afraid." I hung up.

~

Roddy and I decided the next step was to tell Naomi Wright that we'd found Samson Henderson. That he had changed addresses. That he did not want to see her anymore and that he asked us not to share his address with her.

She objected to the last part.

"Yeah," Roddy said, "we think you'd head over there with a firearm and rape him again. So no, you can't have the address. That ain't happenin'."

"But I love him," Naomi responded.

"It's not a two-way street," I said. "He no longer wants your affections, such as they are. I'm afraid you've been dumped."

She looked at Roddy and then at me. "And he plans to rape someone else?"

Roddy narrowed his eyes. "He says no."

"You know that's a lie."

"Tend to agree with you. Not sure what we can do to stop it."

"Would you arrange it so we could meet? To end it properly? At a neutral place? Like a park?"

Roddy and I agreed we would ask Henderson if he would meet our client one last time. No guarantees. Naomi nodded. She picked a park bench near her apartment, said it was a place where they had once sat and read the newspaper. We nodded and left.

~

Henderson agreed to the meeting. It was scheduled for his first day off which was Sunday. We met Naomi at her apartment. Roddy searched her purse and I patted her down. No problems there. Naomi had no weapons. We walked to the park. Naomi bought a Sunday *Los Angeles Times* on the way, hoping things would go better than what Roddy and I envisioned.

Samson Henderson was a little bit late. As he approached from the parking lot, Roddy met him. The once and future rapist carried nothing and wore cargo shorts, a t-shirt, and grubby carwash tennies. My partner patted him down, verifying all was well. Once we decided he was clean, Roddy cleared out of the way. Henderson joined Naomi on the bench. A few other people were strolling by, joggers or people with dogs as it was only 10 am.

Naomi dominated the conversation. She waved her arms around, gesticulating in moderate fashion. We watched from a sufficient distance to not hear the conversation, giving them a modicum of privacy. But the truth is we didn't want to hear any more about their sick vibe.

Roddy looked at me. "She can't admit that it's over."

I nodded.

Naomi continued to plead. Her face became red. Sammy looked entrenched. Then in a more flamboyant move, Naomi swept her arms up and then down past Henderson. She awkwardly knocked the newspaper from the bench. She bent at the waist and leaned forward toward the sidewalk in front of her to pick up the paper still in its plastic bag roll.

As she bent down, she pulled at something under the bench's seat.

"What the hell..." Roddy said, starting to move toward them, but they were one hundred feet away out of earshot.

I began to run too, but we only had one real leg between us. Roddy moved on two prosthesis and me on one. We are not sprinters. Naomi had time to pull the gun free of the duct taped holster under the bench. She stood with the Glock in her two hands just like she was trained. Henderson likewise stood. He raised his hands. His face showed fear and he was speaking, but we couldn't hear it. Roddy and I had just cut the distance in half before she shot him.

Roddy answered the phone when Speedy Khuzaymah called the office on Monday morning. He handed the receiver to me.

The police detective said, "Hi Grace. Nothing personal, but I prefer to deal with you. Tell Roddy it's a cop thing. You having carried the shield and all."

"Roddy don't mind. What's up?"

"Got news."

"Yeah?"

"Yeah. We interviewed both Henderson and Wright. And both are lying to us. Henderson says he brought the gun. That it was hers and he was returning it. It went off as they were exchanging it and he isn't pressing charges."

"He said that, eh?"

"Yeah, said you and Roddy need to change your statements. That you got it wrong."

"What's his status?"

"Oh, she shot him dead center in the groin, blew his package right off. Made a eunuch out of Sam, she did."

"And he's not pressing charges?"

"No, he's not. And there's more news."

"Really, pray tell what?"

"Sam wants to invite you to the wedding. They're getting married."

I laughed. "That takes balls."

Speedy laughed. "Sam proposed at the prison ward hospital last night through his court appointed attorney. Naomi was in holding when she got the news from her lawyer as well."

"And just when you think you've seen it all," I said, then held the phone aside to tell Roddy the news. "Okay, Speed. Thanks for the update. We'll be down to amend our statements. It was hard to see what was happening at that distance."

Speedy hung up laughing.

I told Roddy the score. He shook his head, moving to the bar in my office to pour us each a shot of Wellers. "Friends with benefits gone wrong," he said.

"Fiends," I said. "Not friends."

"Duly noted," he replied, his voice raspy after a swig of the bourbon. "Which side are you sitting on? Bride or groom?"

"Oh, I'm busy that day."

"When is it?"

"Don't know."

He nodded and poured a second round.

EPILOGUE: AD INFINITUM, AMEN

I t was dawn, New Year's Day. Las Vegas at the Mirage. I heard a buzz. It was my cell phone. I picked up. It was Roddy.

"Happy damn New Year!"

"Back at cha," I said. "It is a little early."

"Yeah, no shit. Got a message, said it was an emergency."

"From whom? I'm out, Rod. I'm not a detective anymore. We both agreed."

"I know," he said, "but Thiago Reyes called. Said for you to call on a secure line. Said you should buy a new burner. He sounded paranoid as hell."

Thiago Reyes was L.A.'s oldest gangbanger. He was head of the Latin Playboys and a ruthless crime boss. I nodded, looking across the bed to see Linda still sleeping. It had been a late night and we had not been asleep all that long.

"I'll call him," I said and hung up.

I got dressed and descended to the street. The lobby casino was deserted, but the Vegas strip is never completely abandoned. And it is always open for business. I stopped at a bodega inside a shaky looking streetside mall. I spotted some cheap phones for sale under the counter.

I asked the clerk, "How much for a burner?"

"Two hundred."

It was a ridiculous price, but I took out two Benjamins and a twenty for tax.

"You need minutes?"

"Yeah, that's extra?"

"One hundred minutes, twenty more."

"Why not?" I said and plunked down another twenty.

"Now must register with driver's license," he said. "I tell criminal types that Kansas does not allow Nevada to verify driver's license numbers, but we still accept them."

I smiled. "Coincidentally I am from Kansas, and I evidently look the criminal type."

The clerk smiled wryly. I wrote, "Kansas #123456789" on the line and signed my name, "Richard Nixon."

The clerk looked down and nodded. "You are lucky. Easy number to remember." He took the form and handed me the phone in a plastic bag.

On the street, I made the call to Thiago Reyes.

Thiago answered on the first ring.

"You on a new phone?"

"Yes, you sound paranoid. What's wrong?"

"You know an LAPD detective named Fernando Vega?"

"Yeah, Robbery and Homicide Division. He investigated the Carson Citizen's bank job. Badly. Why?"

"Vega doesn't like you."

I laughed. "The line is long. 'Inna Gadda Da Vida' long."

It was Reyes' turn to laugh. "You lucky I'm old. That is a really old reference."

"What about Vega?" I asked, returning us to topic.

"He don't like you. Vega put word on the street he thinks you have committed murder. Offered ten large for evidence or testimony to put you on ice."

"And you're worried because we scratched each other's back way back when?"

"I trust you, but I know you had help with the Russians. Anton Talonov."

I thought of Rat. "My associate will never spill. You don't do your own dirty work. What about your helpers on Mariyah Nadim? They secure?"

"They both dead. So, I feel certain they keep quiet."

"The two of us have forgotten the entire episode," I said.

"Okay. You got any other skeletons in the closet? Vega wants your hide on the wall."

I laughed again. "Thiago, you watching old westerns again?"

"Reading Louis L'Amour. Like those Sackett stories."

"Yeah, gotcha," I said. "I left L.A. Thiago, I'm out. Vega just gonna have to get over his snit. I don't have the time to run detective tutorials for him."

"Detective work is like gangsta life. No getting out."

"I'm going to try."

"I got you on retainer, Detective Pancake. You owe me. Your partner, Stumpy, gonna take me on? I got concerns in this city of angels. I can't quit. I got an empire to run. Only way out for us bangers is in a box,"

"Sometimes L.A.'s dead get buried out in the Sonora."

"Nah, my enemies wouldn't go to the trouble. We curb-side." He laughed grimly.

"Keep living, Thiago."

"You too. Want me to call you I hear more about Vega?"

"No, don't."

He hung up. I took the battery out of the phone and threw it and the phone into the sewer grate. The air was beginning to warm. It was a new day. Linda and I planned on a good ride. The future loomed. But the road still offered freedom. Ad Infinitum. Amen.

TUNES FOR GOODBYE

Bad Luck, Blue Eyes, Goodbye – Black Crowes

Leaving the Monsters Behind – The Jayhawks

This Side of Goodbye – Eric Burdon and the Animals

Living in a Ghost Town – The Rolling Stones

Never Can Say Goodbye – Isaac Hayes

Goodbye Pork Pie Hat – Jeff Beck

Forever is Ending Today – Ernest Tubb

Too Late for Goodbyes – Julian Lennon

Kiss and Say Goodbye – Joan Osborne

Goodbye Girl – Squeeze

Leaving Trunk – Taj Mahal

Goodbye Stranger – Supertramp

Shiva Descending – C. S. Angels

Then You Can Tell Me Goodbye – The Casinos

Na Na Hey Hey Kiss Him Goodbye – Steam

We Got to Get Out of This Place – The Animals

Thinking About Leaving – Dwight Yoakam

You've Got to Move – The Rolling Stones

The End of My Run – David Corley

Something Just Ain't Right – Earl Scruggs and Friends

Why Must the Ending Always Be So Sad? – The Flying Burrito Brothers

Rendezvous with the Blues – Gregg Allman

Send Me to the 'Lectric Chair – Hugh Laurie

The Highway is for Heroes – Jesse Colin Young

Please Don't Tell Me How the Story Ends – Joan Osborne

ALSO BY ROCK NEELLY

Novels by Rock Neelly

The Salt Fork Stations

River of Tears

The Purple Heart Detective Agency

The Prince of the Border

A Brand New Me (novella)

Short Story Collections

Babylon Blues (Cases from the Purple Heart Detective Agency)

The Big Jangle (More Case Files from the Purple Heart Detective Agency)

An Anagram for Goodbye

ACKNOWLEDGMENTS

Writing a book is not a solitary act. Lots of people make it good or bad. Hopefully, this manuscript is a good one. A couple of the stories have been part of online promos. *Brand New Me* was published as a standalone novella, but only about three people read it. The readers will judge the final product for themselves. I am proud of it.

I would like to thank Tallie Davis for the great edit. Tony Acree, my publisher, is so great. He puts up with a lot of strange requests and ideas from me. Thanks, brother.

Since I may never have two books with the same release date again, I want to do something a bit off here. I want to thank the authors who molded me through their excellence:

The first, of course, is Jack Olsen, whose amazing skills served as my inspiration that someone could make a living at this game.

My first adult read would have been the swashbuckling books of Alexandre Dumas.

Those were quickly followed by the rollicking tales of Louis L' Amour. I remember my first read being *Down the Long Hills* in the dim light of a music assembly at my mother's school--kids singing on stage while I was mesmerized and transported to the high plains of Colorado.

Soon I found my genre of detective fiction. Raymond Chandler was the keystone. I reread *The Big Sleep* ever so often to remind myself what can be achieved-- the detective novel as literature.

Of course, Graham Greene followed. I read *The Quiet American* in college for Modern British Literature. After my advisor, Jerry Moran, put me into Accounting, I secretly dropped it and took the lit class. A great decision to this day. Greene is the guidepost for me these days. The best writer of the twentieth century for my buck.

My favorite mystery? *Rebecca* by Daphne du Maurier.

My favorite book overall? Hmmm, I will mention three:

A River Runs Through It by Norman Mclean; *Illusions* by Richard Bach; and *Brideshead Revisited* by Evelyn Waugh.

I reread the Waugh book frequently just to hear his exquisite sentences echo in my head.

Favorite detective series? John D. MacDonald's Travis McGee books are hard to beat, but I'll go with Michael Connelly. He ain't Raymond Chandler, but the longevity of his excellence is mind-blowing.

Lyle Lovett once wrote, "And there are more I remember, and more I could mention than words I could write in a song..." and that is apt here. My admiration for authors is enormous. Tip of the hat to them all.